MW01194765

'We're all the same fucking ocean.
We are the same ocean in different drops.'
Peace Chattiya Sinsomboon
(One night on the kerb outside The Bearded Tit)

'We stand on the shoulders of giants whose pain
we will never fully understand.'
Imbar Amira Nassi
a.k.a. imbi
(One night on the couch at Sabrina)

A

LANGUAGE

OF

LIMBS

Through researching and talking about this novel, I learnt how deeply LGBTQIA+ liberation movements are indebted to the resistance and relentless activism of Aboriginal and/or Torres Strait Islander People – a fight that has been fought since invasion, and that continues today. I acknowledge, too, that LGBTQIA+SB People have existed here, and loved here, since time immemorial.

I used to think of my work as an author as something I *did*, not something I *lived*. But through many yarns over the years, especially with Thunghutti and Bundjalung man, Warren Roberts and our friends at Yarn, I have come to understand storytelling as a way of being in the world and acknowledge Aboriginal and Torres Strait Islander People as the First and Original Storytellers and recognise their storytelling as survival, as resistance, as connection to culture, as joy, and as a way to care for Country.

I pay my respects to Elders past and present.

And extend those respects to any Aboriginal and/or Torres Strait Islander People here reading this novel. Sovereignty has never been ceded. Always was, always will be, Aboriginal Land, Water and Sky.

Acknowledgement of Country

I was born in Cammeraygal Country, and have spent the majority of my life living between Gadigal Land, Wangal Land, and Bidjigal Land. I wrote this novel on the lands of the Bundjalung People and swam or surfed, each day after writing, in waters as clear as daylight. This novel is indebted to those rivers and lakes and sea, and to the Bundjalung People who have cared for those waterways since time immemorial, because it was in those waters that I dreamt and was playful, that I grieved, cried and laughed, as I mapped the contours of this novel.

At the time of writing this acknowledgement,
I am living in Gadigal Country.

The First Nations People in my life have taught me so much about place, and what it means to be anchored in land, for our bodies to be rooted in water and sky. I am indebted to these friends for teaching me to slow down and to form deep and lasting relationships. As my dear friend, Larrakia and Jingili woman, Morgan Mags Marlow says, 'You live *in* Country, not *on* it.'

I wish to acknowledge, then, the Traditional Custodians of the Country *in* which I've lived, and pay my deepest respects to the Traditional Custodians of Country right across this vast land and its surrounding islands. I acknowledge those who have been caring for these lands, waters and skies since time immemorial, and the Custodians of today who continue to care for Country and live in enduring connection to culture, despite ongoing processes of brutal and violent colonisation.

A
LANGUAGE
OF
LIMBS

DYLIN HARDCASTLE

DUTTON

DUTTON

An imprint of Penguin Random House LLC
1745 Broadway, New York, NY 10019
penguinrandomhouse.com

First published in hardcover in Australia by Picador, an imprint of
Pan Macmillan Australia, Sydney, in 2024.
First American edition published in the United States by Dutton Books,
an imprint of Penguin Random House LLC, in 2025.

Copyright © 2024 by Dylin Hardcastle
Penguin Random House values and supports copyright. Copyright fuels creativity, encourages
diverse voices, promotes free speech, and creates a vibrant culture. Thank you for buying an
authorized edition of this book and for complying with copyright laws by not reproducing,
scanning, or distributing any part of it in any form without permission. You are supporting
writers and allowing Penguin Random House to continue to publish books for every reader.
Please note that no part of this book may be used or reproduced in any manner for the
purpose of training artificial intelligence technologies or systems.

DUTTON and the D colophon are registered trademarks of Penguin Random House LLC.

LIBRARY OF CONGRESS CATALOGING-IN-PUBLICATION DATA

Names: Hardcastle, Dylin, author.
Title: A language of limbs / Dylin Hardcastle.
Description: First American edition. | [New York]: Dutton, 2025.
Identifiers: LCCN 2024052245 (print) | LCCN 2024052246 (ebook) |
ISBN 9780593852736 (ebook) | ISBN 9780593852712 (hardcover)
Subjects: | LCGFT: Queer fiction. | Bildungsromans. | Novels.
Classification: LCC PR9619.4.H363 (ebook) | LCC PR9619.4.H363 L36 2025 (print) |
DDC 823/.92 23/eng/20250—dc13
LC record available at https://lccn.loc.gov/2024052245

International edition ISBN: 9798217046355

Printed in the United States of America
1st Printing

The authorized representative in the EU for product safety and compliance is Penguin Random
House Ireland, Morrison Chambers, 32 Nassau Street, Dublin D02 YH68, Ireland,
https://eu-contact.penguin.ie.

For those who I have loved quietly

trigger warning

THIS NOVEL CONTAINS depictions of family violence, overt transphobia, homophobia, racism and physical violence. This novel portrays the AIDS pandemic. This novel also depicts a stillbirth.

Aboriginal and Torres Strait Islander People are advised that this novel contains references to the Stolen Generations and police brutality.

I have done my best to accurately portray the lived experiences of the LGBTQIA+ community in a time I didn't live through. However, I acknowledge that the LGBTQIA+ community is not a monolith, and that it is full of vastly diverse experiences. Thank you to those who have offered guidance and consultation. I hope I have done this story justice.

Most of all, I hope that as you read, you feel our joy.

limb one

ALL MY LIFE, undoes.

With my t-shirt – discarded on the floor. With my flesh – pricked pink and glistening in the hot glow of the lamp. With my breath – dense as a downpour. With my hips – pressed hard against the workbench. With my spine – arced and shivering. With my throat – open. With her hand – inside me. With our mouths – ravenous. With the door behind us – opening to the impervious wall of night. All my life, undoes.

Because my mother, standing in the doorway of the garden shed, *screams*. Or at least, that's how I'll remember it. A scream that pierces and pulls apart. Her words all blurring together, because I am already underwater.

I feel the blood draining from my hands and feet, running back into my core to protect my heart. I feel weightless, yet impossibly here, because there's no escaping. There's only undoing.

She has put her clothes back on.

Get dressed, she says, here, put this on! She thrusts my t-shirt in my lap. I clutch the shirt, for a breath, and feel this moment stretch out sideways, as I look through my own tears into her eyes, this girl I love, shaking my head, crying inside, *no, no, no!* As she manages a smile and squeezes my shoulders and my limbs quake like they already know what I'm about to lose. Because she leaves, pushing past my mother, out into the darkness. Running off down the street. I will never see her again. She is gone.

My father has heard the scream, and by the time he finds my mother, I am a shuddering, shaking. Trembled mess. My mother is in the doorway, pointing at me. What is it? he asks, hands open and reaching for me. Are you okay? And for a moment, I think I am saved. Forgiven. A moment – passes.

She was, my mother starts, struggling for words, with *her*. I scramble to my feet. Dad, wait, please. His eyes dart between my mother and me. I'm in my cotton shirt and pyjama pants. He looks down at my bare feet. The garden shed smells of wood shavings and compost and flesh. What the hell is going on? he asks, face fattening with frustration. Your daughter . . . says my mother, looking away from me, her face contorted by repulsion, like she can no longer fathom that I am of her. She was touching that girl! *Touching?* Oh, come on! My mother shrieks, erupts with tears. For God's sake! She was kissing that *slut*!

That single word is an axe. Heart hacked into bloody chunks. Because this summer rolled through me like black thunder, hot and heaving. And she witnessed me in strikes of lightning. Flashes of truth and ecstasy. With her, my naked body shifted from an object of desire to the subject of the story. She saw me in all my horror, my blood sparkling red, staining her fingers the first time she reached inside me. And I liked how it felt, being turned inside out, learning that the self becomes whole in the moment it is opened.

I watch now, my hands on my mother's chest, shoving her body, as if they are someone else's hands. My mother's head hits the shed wall so hard I think she might break through it. Her lips round into an O as a rush of air leaves her throat. Winded, she gasps. I watch her floundering in a pool of shock and disgust. My father's hands are around my neck before I think to run. He drags me through the door, out onto the back lawn. And in the soft glow of the porch light, I see my father's face, the colour of a salmon belly sliced open. Fleshy and wild. I try to speak, but his grip holds all the words. He raises his fist. Hesitates.

I think, I might die here.

The blow is swift. Cold on my face the way ice almost feels hot. I land flat on my back. The earth beneath me is spinning but spinning the other way. The wrong way.

I breathe in the sweetness of freshly cut grass. Inside muscle, the scent becomes the stench I will forever associate with the last time I see my father. Because as he kneels for another strike, I roll and scramble to my feet. He grabs my ankle, yanks me back. I kick him in the face, feel his nose crunch beneath my heel. He lets go and I am free. Up and running. Through the side gate. Down the driveway. Barefoot on concrete. I run and run and run until my feet are bleeding and I'm collapsing into the beginning of what will be my after. Because I know already that I'll never again sleep in that bed, or swim in that pool, or piss in that toilet, or eat at that table. I'll never again be between the borders of that house, because my *being* is transgression. A ghost there now, slipping through the plaster and weatherboard. Bleeding on the grass. Seeped into earth. I'll exist in that house only as an echo of everything before.

All my life . . . Here it is. Undone.

limb two

I WAKE IN a heave of breath, reach for my bedside lamp and pull the string.

Between my legs, I feel the wet of my underwear.

Behind my eyes, I recall her – me, us – with startling realness, as if it were a memory. And perhaps it is. A memory of a memory of a yearning. Because in this dream –

she's on her back – a white singlet – shadows of pink – I am grinding – her hands on my hips guiding me – back and forth and back and forth – mouth ajar – breath shuttling – she makes sounds I haven't heard before – sounds that excite me – sounds that make my heart flutter like starling wings – like a great migration – south – a murmuration in the sky – swelling and contracting – the room is dark and blurry at the edges – everything is burning aching deep inside – and it feels good, this ache – a pulsation making me feel that I am alive – I am alive! – together – we bend and arc and grind in the unmoored glow – I look up – see the ceiling dissolve and fall away – light avalanches in – my eyes adjust and her face comes into focus – *her* – her since five years old – her since knobbly knees and missing teeth – her since the beginning of memory – time – desire – her – here – here she is –

I let out a deep sigh. Thinking of all the dreams. So many dreams, one after another, calcifying in the shape of her body. I remember her nipples hard beneath her singlet. I remember the sounds she made. I remember the unmoored glow. And all I want is to forget.

Because there she is – asleep on the pull-out mattress on the floor of my bedroom. I look down at my best friend, her still body, washed by tender light. Her face is dreaming soft. I watch her sleeping in this moment that feels swollen and wide as a lake.

Then slowly, I reach for the lamp, pull the string and turn off the light. Plunge back into darkness.

limb one

THERE'S A COMMUNITY park where I used to play with the boys in my suburb. Back when I was kicking the footy and getting tackled and jumping out of trees, just like them. Back when I had cropped hair and taut skin, just like them. Back before my body swelled and they became scared to tackle me, worried about hurting a girl. Back before I became the pulse of their desire. Suddenly watched. Suddenly craved.

I don't realise that I'm back in this park until the sky whitens and the spray-painted lines of the footy field take shape. I'm sitting against the trunk of a Moreton Bay fig overlooking the park. The tree's skin is ribbed, veiny, cold. I wonder how old it is. It has been here for as long as I can remember, with its wide crown and huge, slumped arms. A kookaburra swoops down from the sky, landing on a branch above me. I crane my neck to look up at it, perched just above my head. I sit still and quiet, not wanting to scare it away, as day slowly breaks all around us. I imagine what my face must look like in the quickening light. One eye swollen shut. The throb of my flesh is an anchor hooked into the dirt of the present. I am held here by this pain, sharp-edged and metallic.

I remember how I felt the first time I sat with her by the still water of the creek, how everything became rippled and saline. How she had laughed at my nervousness. How I'd laughed at hers. How we witnessed each other. Suddenly, the kookaburra begins to laugh. The sound, fresh feathered and glittering, reverberates out through the park, into this new day. It feels cruel and absurd and beautiful.

limb two

My mum is awake when I walk through the kitchen. Morning, honey, she says and kisses me on the cheek. Did you sleep okay?

I shrug. Kind of . . . I had weird dreams.

Oh dear, again? What were they about?

I tell her I don't remember.

We eat breakfast at the family table, and I try not to look my best friend in the eyes. Because after years of her harbouring my secrets, she has become the key that might unlock me. Her eyes, dark brown and bordered by thick lashes, see me. Really see me. And I'm terrified of what she sees. Of what she might know. Of what she might suspect. So, I shove pancakes into my mouth and try to forget how I feel with her lips wet against mine.

She wants to swim in the pool.

It's a cracking day, my dad says.

We get changed in my room. I face the wall, partially hiding behind my cupboard door, and she laughs and tells me, oh, come on, I've seen it all before. And she has. From the swelling of my breasts to the growth of hair between my legs. She's seen it all before, as I have seen all of her. And yet, the flesh of this world feels sparkling and new. Like a sheet of ice glistening on the underside of the earth, changing every season, so that even when you've mapped it end to end, the contours of the coast take on a new shape and everything you think you knew becomes part of *before*.

There's an orange flowering gum that overhangs my family's pool. The sun falls through it, landing on the water, flecking it with sap-green light. I dive in first. It's autumn and the water is already cold, engulfing my body. Dad is sitting in a deckchair, reading the paper. He tells us, somewhat proudly, that he has changed the chemical he ordinarily puts in, to a magnesium chlorine mixture.

The magnesium makes the water feel like silk.

She jumps in, knees tucked, cannonball. Surfaces laughing, splashing about. I am floating on my back. I can hear her talking about an assignment we have coming up. Then she says something about Greg, the guy she has a crush on. I exhale and sink, though I don't know I'm sinking. Not until my back lands on the pool floor. I open my eyes. The surface is a metre above me. Beyond that, the flowering gum bends its limbs in a gentle breeze. My lungs begin to burn.

I think, I might die here.

My best friend is here for the entire weekend, until her parents return from their vineyard in the Hunter Valley. And though

I come up from the bottom of the pool, I don't really breathe again, not until she's back next door. Waving over the fence. See you at school!

At school, she tells our friends about our weekend full of my mum's delicious food and my dad's shitty jokes and splashing about in the pool. All I can remember in any detail is the feeling of lying a metre underwater, choked by my desire.

Greg is standing down the street while we're waiting for the bus. One of the girls tells her to go speak to him. Ask him to the dance!

Oh no, she says, blushing, I couldn't. I'm too scared! And then she looks at me. Can you say something?

My insides lurch. *What?*

Please! You're my best friend. Go tell him . . . I don't know! She laughs. Just make me sound cool!

I am shaking, but I say, okay.

Slowly, I feel myself settle into a cold determination. Push my shoulders back. I can hear giggling behind me. She is excited. Thrilled, even, because she knows me, she knows I'll tell him she's the best thing ever. That she's mind-blowingly smart. *She knows every capital city of every country! Seriously! Just ask her.* That I'll tell him that she laughs with her whole body. How it makes everyone else laugh with her. That I'll say that she eats fish because she likes to think the whole ocean then exists inside of her, like she's got scales for skin.

Greg is smoking a cigarette. He exhales a thick cloud of smoke, then passes the cig to his friend, Keith. They both go to the boys' school across the road.

Hey, Greg says. Half smiling.

Hi.

Do you want a drag? Keith asks.

Sure, I say, and take the cigarette. I inhale, feel my lungs fill, then exhale. My breath quivers, but, surprisingly, I don't cough.

Greg smiles now, like I've passed some sort of test.

I think, for a moment, of my dream, of my memory of a memory of a desire. Of her panting in my ear. I wince at the bright flashes of her face, lips wet, teeth gleaming. Of our bodies naked and knotted in a room with no edges. I shudder. All I want is to be excised of this haunting.

And so, I take a deep breath and I tell him, I . . . I think we should go to the dance together.

His eyes open wider. Really?

Yeah, I say, taking another drag. The cigarette is nearing its end. It burns hot against my fingers. I throw it on the ground and stamp it out with my shoe.

Keith is looking from me to Greg, trying to gauge his friend's response.

Okay, he says. Sure.

I brush his hand with my fingertips. I feel nothing.

Do you want to kiss me? I ask. Greg shrugs, then nods, and I take hold of his hand, drawing it to my hip. I arc my neck back. He leans down. Up close I see the wispy hairs sprouting from his upper lip and chin. I close my eyes and find his mouth. Greg's lips are cracked from the sea. He tastes of tobacco and spiced chewing gum.

I sit next to him on the back seat of the bus the whole way home. I kiss him on the cheek when the bus reaches my stop. See you soon, I say, and he grins. When I pass her, there are tears in her eyes and she looks at me, searching. I like that to her, I am a stranger now. I like that she hates me. Because, I realise, hate and love sometimes come wrapped up and intertwined. It's easier, this way.

limb one

THERE IS SOMETHING I soon learn about time . . . I learn that it stretches and slows and becomes difficult to fill when you have nowhere to go.

I think of ending things.

There is a new shopping precinct in town. I don't believe my mother shops here. She doesn't drive, and it's several suburbs away from ~~our~~ . . . *her* house, so I think, hope, I might be safe here.

I walk into a clothing store, find a pair of shoes in my size. Some socks. A jumper. The shop assistant is helping an elderly woman try on a pair of boots. I walk out with everything. It's just one bare foot in front of the other until I'm out of the shop, down the street and around the corner, clutching all that I have. It's all that I have. I sit down in the gutter, dust the gravel off my feet and put on my new socks. My feet are all cut up. The cotton sticks to the pus. It stings a little, but when I put the trainers on, they cushion my feet like smoke, luxuriously soft after hours walking barefoot on hot bitumen.

Now what?

My stomach growls and I try not to think of my mother's pancakes. How she'd make them on Sunday mornings when I had friends staying over. Stacks of them, fluffy and golden, with strawberries soaked in maple syrup. I try not to think of my father's barbecues, the whole street packed into our backyard. Rissoles and sausages sizzling on the grill. Licked by tongues of fire. My mother, yelling at him, it's too hot! Turn it down! as she and the other women lay out a spread of apricot chicken and devilled eggs. Prawn cocktail on a bed of iceberg lettuce. All those neighbours, packed into the backyard, with dogs barking and kids cannonballing into the pool. What will my parents say next time?

I imagine my father standing by the barbecue, tongs in his hand, and my mother, hanging off his arm. She'll flick her hair back off her shoulder and say, with pride, we've sent her to a boarding school. In Melbourne, my father will add. And my mother will smile as she boasts, she's just too bright for the schools here.

In another version, my parents will chop me out of all the family photographs. My father will repaint my room and take my clothes to the tip, tossing them in a heap between the rats and rotten mattresses. But not my journals or my art. My collages. My paintings. My Polaroids of a summer spent between yellow banksias. Her. Her body all saturated and dripping. My love letters. The beginning of everything I dreamt of making. Those, my mother will burn. Our daughter, she will say, is dead.

I walk to Merewether Beach, the sandy edge where the steel city of Newcastle meets the Tasman Sea. Along the horizon, huge ships with shining red hulls await their turn in the harbour.

Standing atop the grassy knoll above the beach, I watch two surfers walk up through the bushy dunes and rinse the salt off under a public shower. They are only a few years older than me, I guess, with their sun-bleached hair and chapped lips. Still lanky and lean. I watch them chatting, laughing. What are they saying, I wonder. One cocks his head to the side, fingering his ear to get the water out. When he straightens his neck, he sees me staring and looks, for a moment, puzzled. Then he grimaces. I avert my gaze and start walking down the path towards the beach. I feel his eyes hooked into my shoulder blades, hear him snickering with his friend. Quicken my pace.

Bronzed bodies are splayed out on the sand on brightly coloured towels. The beach smells of coconut tanning oil and dried seaweed. I take off my shoes and jumper. It's autumn, but the air is still hot. I sink my feet into the sand – coarse and crunching under my weight. Sitting down, I scoop up a handful, letting it sift slowly through my fingers, time landing in a small mound of broken bodies.

I don't have swimmers, so I strip down to my t-shirt and undies. People are looking at me, I think. Then I realise, no, they're not. None of them. Because they have gossip and chitchat and catch-ups, and books to read and children to watch in the water. They have lives that exist here and now. And none of them knows that I can't go home. That I have no home. That I loved my best friend and now I might die.

The ocean takes me. Like the sea is real and all that was a bad dream. Like the shore will take a different shape when I touch the sand again. Like I'll be able to go back to my bed and dream a new dream. I dive under and open my eyes. From here, the world is sun-lanced and shimmering green. I swim through beams of soft light, my body turned over by clouds of sea foam. I feel weightless. Effortless.

I think of ending things. Because when I return to shore, the fabric of my t-shirt has stretched. Sopping wet, it sticks and clings to all the awkward parts of my flesh. I feel overdressed and foolish. But this is the normal bit, to be fifteen years old and self-conscious of my half-formed breasts and meaty thighs. I can stomach *this* bit. It's that *other* bit I can't. It's the walking slowly, the not wanting to reach my clothes on the sand because when I put them on, what else is there?

I don't even have a towel.

limb two

I AM EXILED from my friendship group, but I survive, because I have a boyfriend now and the dreams have stopped.

I spend recess and lunchtime in the school library. The air is stuffy, but the librarians know me by name, and on Wednesday, they share their morning tea cake with me. Here, I get to exist between books. Tiny worlds open up to me and become big. I go somewhere else, into the blackened woods of old fairytales, into the blinding white of future stars. I read and read and read.

What do you think you'll do after school? Annie asks me one recess, sitting down in the chair beside me. She's silver-haired with hexagonal glasses and pastel-coloured cardigans she tells me she knits herself. I shrug. I'm not sure yet.

Well, what do you like?

I like reading, I tell her.

Annie smiles and says, me too.

I look down at the book I'm reading. A story about slippages, where time falls away and unravels so quickly you feel the wind of it passing through you. I put my bookmark in between the pages and close the book. *Orlando.*

You know, Annie says, Virginia Woolf wrote that book for her lover . . .

Leonard, I say. I'm familiar with their story.

No, Annie says, shaking her head, whispering now. Her name was Vita.

I don't finish *Orlando.* I put it back on the shelf, forgetting to remove my bookmark. And there it will sit, punctuated by a piece of fabric embroidered with my name. Half-known truths. Half-known stories with endless endings.

Three decades will pass before I read another book by Virginia Woolf.

The school dance is on Friday night. Greg comes to my house early to have dinner with my parents. He arrives as Mum lays her apricot chicken on the table. The meat is steaming, glistening and gluggy. When I meet him at the door, he's wearing high-waisted corduroy pants, a white belt and a freshly ironed shirt. His hair is combed over and slicked with gel. I kiss him on the doorstep, then lead him inside.

Mum gives him a hug and tells him how nice it is to finally meet him.

Dad shakes his hand and comments on Greg's firm grip. He's impressed, and says something about Greg being a real man.

Greg is beaming.

Me, I feel like the lino floor is too slippery, like I should step carefully or my feet might slide out from underneath me.

Dad offers Greg a beer, which he readily accepts.

Mum says I can have a glass of wine and pours me one before I agree.

Dad tells Greg that I've never had a boyfriend. I was worried, he says, that she wasn't interested in boys! My face flushes. Hot pink. I feel so big with all their eyes on me.

Oh, stop that nonsense! my mother says, laughing.

Greg, who is a year older than me, has his licence. He is driving his dad's Holden. The car smells of leather and tobacco. He lights a cigarette, then passes it to me. I take a drag while he inserts his new cassette into the car's stereo. 'I Want to Hold Your Hand', by The Beatles comes through the speakers. The sound crackles and pops, but we don't notice, because we're singing too loudly. When the song ends, I say, you're a terrible singer.

He laughs from the back of his throat. So are you!

And now I am laughing too. Because this is easy, belting out a chorus about things I understand.

We meet Keith and two more of Greg's friends, Darren and Paul, in an alleyway beside the community hall. Darren is with his girlfriend, Helen, who is in my year, but at another school in Newcastle.

Greg introduces us.

It's nice to meet you, she says, then compliments my skirt.

Thanks, I say, blushing. My mum made it.

Greg has his arm around my shoulder. Should we go in? he asks.

We head to the door, where a parent is taking coin donations.

Greg pulls out two coins, saying he's paying for me, even though I have a coin that my mum gave me. Thanks, I say, smiling.

He tells me, no worries, then plants a kiss on my cheek.

Greg can't sing, but surprisingly, he can dance. And for a moment, I am swept up in the way his long limbs bend and sway with perfect rhythm. He grabs me by the hips and pulls me into the song, into its beat. I dance with him guiding me, and all the awkwardness falls away. And I think, *this* is exciting. *This* is how I'm supposed to feel.

Then I see her, moving across the dance floor like a swell undulating through open ocean, and the ceiling opens up for me to shiny wet sky. I want to touch her, to rise and fall with her. And so I say to Greg, should we get out of here?

He nods, grinning widely.

Keith, Paul, Darren and Helen squish into the back of Greg's dad's Holden. I'm in the front with Greg. We drive with the windows down, air rushing in between plumes of cigarette smoke, all the way to Merewether Beach. Greg parks by the surf club. We get out and walk down to the edge of our town, where the lights of houses and streetlamps spill out into black water.

We take off our shoes and clothes on the sand and sprint into the darkness, screaming and splashing about. Greg finds me in the sea and kisses me hard, his naked body pressed up against mine. His tongue is warm salt.

There's a faint pulsation between my legs, and the longer he kisses me, the thicker it becomes. So much so that I almost forget the shore of my desire.

We lie between tufts of grass and crab holes. I'm on my back. We don't have a towel. His body is on top of mine, and as he finds his way inside me, I exhale all the parts of me that imagined something else.

limb one

My sixteenth birthday passes through me unknowingly. I have my head in a dumpster when I find a newspaper with the date on it: *28 April 1972*. Four days have passed since the garden shed. Or is it five? Six?

Happy birthday to me, I say.

I wonder how the day passed through my parents. Strangely, imagining that they had cared is so much more painful. I realise that hate and love sometimes come wrapped up and intertwined.

I fish from the dumpster two brown bananas and a cookie tin. Prying the tin open, I find, to my sheer joy, Arnott's assorted biscuits. They're stale, but I don't care. As I shove the first into my mouth, I can't help but laugh at the irony. My mother, too, would have thrown these away, never allowing anything to go stale in her kitchen. It's mothers like her prematurely throwing things out that allows for daughters like me to survive.

I crouch down behind the bin and ram biscuit after biscuit into my mouth, barely chewing, so they form thick wads in my throat. Down the alleyway, a girl walks past in her school uniform. She turns her head and I lean into the shadow of the bin.

I think of school. Chalk words and diagrams on the blackboard are already beginning to warp and fade, becoming memories of a memory. Yet the feeling of being in the library, surrounded by shelves of books, feels achingly fresh. When I remember that the book I was reading, *Orlando*, will now sit on the shelf indefinitely, half finished, I am overcome by grief. In these half-known truths, there are endless endings, and I mourn the open-ended ending of everything I ever knew. Perhaps that's how endings happen. We like to think of full stops and final pages, but so often the book is forgotten or lost, leaving us on a half-formed thought with nothing to close the

A rat scurries past me. I shriek and jump to my feet, looking back down the alleyway. The girl is gone. Just like that. Off on her way to school.

When I wake in the afternoon, I pick up my biscuit tin and walk. Down the alleyway. Along the street. A school bus turns a corner. More school kids. I feel a pang of anxiety because, once upon a time, the school bus was the only place I found it difficult to survive. School was fine. I was good at school, excellent even. Surely good enough to get a university scholarship.

I paid attention in class and handed in my homework ahead of time. A teacher's pet. A nerd. A freak, because I spent recesses and lunches in the library, alone. Reading poetry and writing, thinking one day one day one day. The school bus was the twenty hot, sticky minutes that bookended each day. The time when I sat, sweaty, telling myself if I was quiet, maybe they wouldn't know.

Did *I* even know?

I remember how nothing necessarily felt wrong, until it suddenly felt right. How I'd kissed a boy at a school dance and thought, well, that was something. How I was high off the nerves and mistook the feeling for excitement. How it wasn't until I kissed her, down by the creek, all murky water and mangroves, that I understood.

I exist,
    otherwise.

That I felt out of time because everyone else's was circling forward, while mine was beating backwards. The library and the classes and the school bus and the dinner table all became a kind of dream that I sleepwalked through. At night, when I would meet her in the garden shed, I woke up.

Like seeing a painting upside down, trying to make sense of it. Appreciating it, even. Until the painting is inverted and the image becomes crystal clear. Now I can't even remember what the world looked like before it made sense.

Another school bus is approaching. It's this easy, I think, to obliterate oneself. I take a deep breath and step forward off the kerb.

The bus driver slams on his horn. I jump back as the bus whooshes past. The driver shakes his head at my stupidity, then continues down the street to a future I will never know. A half-known truth. A story with endless endings . . . I can't go back for fear my father might kill me. Or for fear that he might not?

When I picture the alternative – going home, brushing over, pretending none of this ever happened – I think, I *would* rather die. Going back into the upside down feels utterly impossible.

So, I stick out my hand, out of time, thumb up, backwards, until a ute pulls to the kerb and a man with a cigarette hanging out of his mouth winds down the window. Where are you going? he asks. I think of the furthest place I know from here. Brisbane. He says, I'm heading west. I ask, can you take me to the highway? He shrugs. Sure, get in, and reaches across to unlock the passenger door. The cabin reeks of yellowed smoke. Thanks, I say, closing the door. He pulls away from the kerb and tells me his name is Steve, then jokes that his missus would kill him if she saw me in his ute. I ask bluntly, why? Not because I don't know, but because I think it's a stupid thing to say. He laughs, the sound bubbling in his throat. He says something about my black eye, but I'm not listening because his eyes are sliding all over me. I tug at my shorts, stretching the fabric so that it covers my knees. He reaches across and pulls my hand away. The fabric lifts. He grins.

I jump out of Steve's ute as it's rolling to a stop at a traffic light. I trip and land in the gutter. Hear him cackling as he revs the engine behind me. He yells out, prick tease! As I scramble off the road onto long grass that itches, I'm panting, not out of fear, but out of rage. Rage at his seedy smile. Flashed teeth. His hand on my leg. Rage at that ridiculous laugh, like he's king of the highway. I want to kick him in the jaw. To stomp on that stupid grin. I kick a picket fence and scream.

Hey there . . . you alright?

I turn around. A man is walking towards me. Over the sounds of cars whooshing, he says, pretty impressive that was. *Piss off!* I yell, giving him the finger. At that, he steps closer. I look at his thick arms, bloated belly, broad shoulders, fat neck and think, *yeah, I'll give it a shot.* I puff up my chest, becoming huge with air, and clench my fists. He raises both hands above his head. Hey hey hey, he says. I'm not going to fight you. Bloody hell. I scream, *Stay back!* And he does. He stops in his tracks, hands still above his head. I'm Dave, he says, I'm a truck driver. I bring fruit from Queensland down to Sydney. I eye him up and down. He's wearing a suit, pressed shirt and tie. His thin hair is combed to one side. I say, you don't look like a truck driver. Dave looks down at his outfit and chuckles. Yes, well, I've been at a funeral, he says. Then his voice cracks as he tells me, someone I loved . . . someone I loved very much. I notice his pink cheeks, his bloodshot eyes and puffy eyelids. My breathing is sharp, quick ins and outs, but I feel the knots of rage inside me loosening. My body is undoing, undone. I collapse back onto the grass. Let out a big sigh.

Slowly, Dave kneels beside me. I see him take in the sight of my face. He sighs at the bulging blue of my flesh and gently asks me, you got a home? I point to my swollen eye. He nods, silent. Then he says, where are you headed? He's gentle with his words in a way that feels at odds with his meaty body. Where are *you* headed? The laugh that comes out of him is rough, but genuine. I'm going to Sydney, he tells me. Me too, I answer. Well, he says, that's lucky for me. That's my truck . . . He points to a nearby petrol station where a big orange truck is parked. Dave tells me that he's about to drive it back to Sydney and that he could really use the company, after the funeral, and I actually believe him, feeling in my gut that this is okay, that he means it, because his eyes aren't grease rubbed all over my body. His gaze is a still and quiet grey, like a slow sea taking on the colour of clouds.

Dave asks me my name. As I'm about to answer, it dawns on me that I can be anyone. I am everyone and no one. Then, because he's looking at me, anticipating my response, my mind goes blank and I blurt out his name, Dave. He laughs, *ha!* Dave is smiling but he shakes his head. Two Daves, he says. Both going to Sydney. Yeah, I say, holding my breath. Then, he chuckles again and says, what are the chances! And I feel myself relax, perhaps even smile.

The cabin is high up. I feel like I'm spying on unsuspecting drivers, and I guess I am. Dave reaches into the centre console and pulls out a bottle of Coke. Want one, Dave? he says, cracking the lid off the bottle as he drives with his elbows. I remember that I am Dave, that he's talking to me. Yeah, I say, please. Dave passes me the bottle and pulls out a second. There are lollies in there, too, he says. Help yourself. He takes a swig of his Coke. Ahh! he says, patting his round belly. Then he lets out a loud burp. I take a gulp from my bottle. The Coke fizzes in my mouth. I burp too. It burns in my nose. He reaches across and clinks our bottles together. Cheers, Dave! I respond, Cheers, Dave! And then we're both laughing.

Out the window, wide stretches of bush rush past in strokes of green and burnt umber. Crossing a plateau, I take in the enormity of the land beyond, folds of mountain like sun-drenched shoulders. And the Hawkesbury River, curved and pulsating like an artery. I know I'll never go back to Newcastle. The road winds between walls of exposed rock and towering gums, and I realise that most endings happen to us. That often, you don't know the last word will be the last until it already has been. Handing in a school assignment. Getting a hug from my mother. Sleeping in the only bed I've ever slept in. Kissing her in the shadows of my family home. Feeling her reach deep inside me. You just don't know that the last time is going to be the last time until it already has been.

I place my own full stop.

limb two

GREG DROPS OUT of school and gets a job in the mines. Soon, he buys a car. A Ford Falcon. Says, now we can go wherever we want.

He picks me up from my parents' house and we drive, windows down. Sky rushing in. I look through the windscreen to the road ahead, wondering where it all ends. I feel the road opening fully in front of me, swallowing everything behind me. He touches my leg. Where does it end? I feel a sudden desire to be there, at the end, at the dead end, where two kerbs close. The dead end of all this.

Greg drives down a track to the dirt car park at the edge of Catherine Hill Bay. The surf is rolling in beyond us. Brown foam in the aftermath of a storm. He tells me what it's like, being underground. How the dirt finds its way in, everywhere. Ears. Nose. Mouth. How he showers at the end of his long shifts and the water runs off him, black on pink tiles. We climb into the back seat of the Ford Falcon, and as he enters me, I imagine I, too, am underground. I am so deep underground that, thankfully, the dreams have ceased. Not even she can find me here.

I turn sixteen. My mother bakes a carrot cake. Greg is here, along with Keith, Darren, Helen and Paul. We're in the pool when Mum and Dad bring the cake out, candles lit. We clamber out of the water, hurriedly drying ourselves as the candles burn closer to the cake. Quick! my mother says, the wax is dripping!

I blow out the candles and wish for a scholarship. Mum passes me a knife and I slice through the thick cake.

Helen giggles, then says, it's dirty! Kiss the closest boy!

Paul quickly gets out of the way, and everyone is laughing. I lean across and kiss Greg on the cheek. They're all clapping and cheering. Dad pats Greg on the shoulder and winks at him, and I see Greg swell with pride.

When I'm helping Mum dust off the tablecloth, she says, I still can't believe you didn't invite her . . . this must be the first birthday party you've had apart.

I tell Mum I don't want to talk about it.

Oh, honey. I'm sure it's not too late to make up.

I pass Mum the tablecloth and walk inside.

I go back to the library. Every day, alone with the books. I do my homework and assignments ahead of time. Then I read . . . everything. From Miles Franklin across the seas to Rebecca West. Eventually, the librarians come to me when they order new books for the shelves. They, of course, have all read more widely than me, and are doing this, I'm sure, to push me into my own expansion. But I like to think they are asking me because I know best.

30

I read Judith Wright, and she turns my attention to the way nature repeats itself, reappearing always in new but familiar iterations. When I go for walks with Mum, I listen to the wind rushing through the trees, and consider how it sounds like wild surf, and how that sound in turn resembles the purr inside a seashell when you lift it to your ear.

I think a lot about words and how they stretch and collapse. I think of how an entire picture is threaded from single, often disparate, strands.

Sometimes I write, but mostly I am crossing out words before the ink has dried.

Judith says that writing is a way of interpreting us to ourselves. And all too often, I fear what might be revealed. So, I read *her* poems, thinking, one day one day one day.

Because when the school bell rings, I shudder. Now that Greg is working and no longer rides the bus home, the bus has become the twenty hot, sticky minutes that bookend each day. She and the girls I used to ride and gossip and laugh with don't speak to me. I am a teacher's pet. A nerd. A freak, because I spend recesses and lunches in the library alone. Some days I go for so long without speaking that the voice in my head grows loud – so loud it sounds as if I am speaking. And maybe I am. Who knows?

One day one day one day.

limb one

I WAKE TO his hand on my shoulder. You right, Dave? he asks. I rub sleep from my eyes. Nod. Yup. He asks, seen this before? I look up through the windscreen at the Sydney Harbour Bridge, arms of steel reaching up up up and across. I think of stories I heard in school, of men all the way up there with fire and hot metal and buckets of water, lobbing smouldering studs from one man to the next. How they fell. Through the air, breaking water with their bodies. Crushed inside out by ocean. I shake my head. Nope. Not in the flesh. See that? he asks, pointing to the top of the bridge where an Australian flag billows in grey wind. Big as this truck, that is. The flag? Dave nods. Bullshit, I say. He laughs, and tells me, perspective changes everything.

The buildings here are taller than anything I've ever seen. I wind down my window and stick my head out. Dave grabs me by the arm and pulls me back into the cabin. Ya wanna get ya head chopped off? I shrug and watch his face change shape.

He sighs . . . Well, he says after a while, shifting gears, I'd prefer it if you didn't. I wind my window back up and wait for him to make a joke about how annoying the mess would be to clean up, but he doesn't.

Hanging from the rearview mirror is a silver locket. I ask him if I can see inside it, and he says sure. Prying the locket open, I see two kids in the left picture and a woman in the right. Those are my kids, Dave says, Andy and Emma. And that there is my wife, Christine. He presses his lips into a smile, then turns back to the road. I look at the small photo of Christine. Her hair is long and black and slick. Her eyes, wet dark. She's smiling. Dimples wedged deep in soft cheeks. She's very beautiful, I say, and Dave's face softens. He nods as if to say, *I know*, though I don't think he means, *I know that she's beautiful*. He knows something else, something deeper, some other truth. And I suddenly feel like I've been sliced open. Dave asks, you ever been in love, Dave? And because of what I'm afraid I'll say next, I just nod silently. He makes a *hm* sound, then asks, had a boyfriend before? I shake my head. Ah, he says. I didn't think so. Then he asks, quieter now, what's her name?

Saying her name, I feel the whole of her pass through my mouth, out between my teeth, across my lips, into the cabin of the truck, out the window, into blue sky. My first and only love. Leaving me. And I know, somehow, that I won't say her name again. Because it hurts too much to yearn for a return.

I resign to her leaving my body, feeling that this is enough. This is enough, to be witnessed by Dave, in the here and now, to have someone in this big wide world know that I loved her. That I loved her. That it was real.

I loved her so much, I say. Dave smiles, nods. Then he says, I'm going to meet some friends for a drink. I think you should come with me . . . if you like?

Dave pulls to the kerb and flicks off the engine. He jumps out of the truck, then comes around to the passenger side to help me down. The street is quiet and lined with terraced houses with flimsy facades. It's all flaky paint, bendy balconies and bruised walls. Weeds sprout through cracks in the concrete. Dilapidated, and yet, something here hums. The air feels charged the way it does before a storm. Behind the concrete and grime, this place is *live*.

We walk until we reach a door painted blue, and as Dave lifts his hand to knock, he turns to me and says, I have a lot of love for my wife.

A man opens the door. He's thin, with gelled hair and bronzed cheekbones. He smiles through glossy lips, kisses Dave on the cheek. Johnny, Dave says, this is Dave. Johnny's eyes flit to me, then back to Dave. *Little* Dave, he adds. Johnny laughs. I guess that makes you *big* Dave, then? Dave smirks, you cheeky bitch. Johnny winks, then turns to me and holds out his hand for me to shake. I notice his nails painted purple, palms smooth, grip gentle. His skin is cool. My name's Johnny, he says. I'm a saltwater man from Larrakia Country. Where you from? I tell him, I was born in Newcastle. Never really been anywhere else. He kisses the top of my hand and says, what a pleasure, Little Dave. Please, come inside.

We descend a set of stairs, narrow as a throat, into the belly of the bar. Dave walks between the tables, nodding his head and smiling at people he seems to know. I meander behind him, hands in my jumper pockets. The sunken room smells of tobacco smoke and spirits and beer-sodden coasters. It's noisy down here, warm and muggy, but not uncomfortable, because something about this place feels like an embrace, like hot breath on skin, like the curve of a caring smile. Like catching your friend's gaze in a crowd and thinking, *oh . . . there you are.*

On the walls, there are black and white photos of men kissing in a time well before mine. There's a framed poster, the word *CAMP* in bold letters, and a flag, pinned in the centre of the wall. Johnny points to it and says, Harold Thomas made this flag. I eye the design, it's made up of two bands of colour – black on top, red beneath, with a yellow circle in the centre. I ask Johnny, what's it for? Johnny smiles and says, darling . . . Then he raises a clenched fist and answers. It's for Aboriginal Land Rights!

On another wall, in bold text, the words,

> GAY POWER
> BLACK POWER
> WOMEN POWER
> STUDENT POWER
> ALL THE POWER TO THE PEOPLE!

I stop before a small photograph in a gold frame. A person with a silver face and bronze arms holds a mirrored orb as they stare down the barrel of the camera. I look at this photograph and feel time spread laterally, becoming wide and open. Like a whole life is being lived inside this small moment. Like there's something in me that recognises . . . myself, perhaps.

Dave smiles and gently coaxes me towards the bar, where a woman who is taller than Dave is drying a glass with a cloth. Her hair is glowing in the haze of red light. Her eyelids shine iridescent blue. She puts down the glass and reaches across the bench to envelop Dave in her arms. She holds him and he softens in her grasp. Like he's letting go of a world inside himself. When she lets go, Johnny says, Daphne, darling . . . this is Little Dave. I step forward, into the bar light, and as Daphne sees my bruised face, she reaches for my hand and says, it's so lovely to meet you, Little Dave.

Johnny walks around behind the bar and pours a shot of whiskey into a short glass. He places it on the bench in front of Dave. Then he pours one for himself, and another for Daphne. How old are you? he asks me. I say, old enough. He raises one eyebrow. Sixteen, I say, and a few days. He laughs and pours me a soda.

We clink drinks, and Johnny says to Dave, hey, you survived. Dave lifts his glass and says, to new beginnings . . .

I notice, in the dim light, that there are tears in Dave's eyes. He blinks and they fall. And it dawns on me that I've never seen a man cry.

So, Little Dave, Johnny says to me, what's your story? Oh, I shrug, I don't have one. Dave tells them that he found me on the street in Newcastle, how he watched me jump out of a car. It all sounds very dramatic, and yet neither Johnny nor Daphne probes for more details. Neither of them asks about my *before* and I begin to understand that in this bar, silences are respected. That there are stories that exist upstairs, outside, that people down here want to repress.

Daphne says, darling, it's a good thing that you're here. I nod, considering that *here* is a place where I might survive. The thought makes me feel like I might burst. With joy. With relief. Like my future is suddenly, in this faint red light, unfolding and possible. I blink and my eyes are a river breaking its banks. Dave puts his hand on my shoulder, and I smile through the wetness and the weight. Johnny asks if I know where I'm going to sleep, and I shake my head. He looks at Daphne, speaking something with his eyes, and she nods and says, of course. Johnny holds my hand and tells me about Uranian House. He says how someone very special, who came from money, bought it in the fifties. That when she died, she left it for her family to look after. And I get the sense that the word *family* means something else in this sentence.

Daphne smiles and says, Little Dave, Uranian House is for people like us.

And this is enough. For me to follow.

Daphne stays at the bar to close, so I leave with Johnny and Dave. We walk through a rain so fine it seems to drift down, slowly and softly, like feathers. Tiny droplets catching on our eyelashes. We walk in and out of light, arriving at last in front of a terrace house three storeys tall. The building is clad in pink with green edges. There's an elaborate wrought-iron fence and huge arched windows. Up on a balcony, two people are smoking cigarettes against the railing. Johnny rifles through the pockets of his denim jacket. Damn, he mutters, then calls out to the people up above, forgot my keys! There is laughter on the balcony. A woman leans over the railing and yells, the sign says no junk males! Johnny snorts. Oh, shut up, Marg! Let us in would ya!

Marg opens the door wearing faded black jeans and a black t-shirt printed with the words *LAND BACK!* across her chest in bold, white letters. She's got her hands on her hips. Her hair is jet-black curls with strands of silver that shimmer in the porch light. She's older than me, by at least two decades. I take in her sharp muscle, her steep collarbones, her sagging breasts, her dark skin, and feel a swelling sense of awe and wonder at the way this woman holds herself. Because when I look at her, I feel like we've been winded, perhaps, by some of the same punches. And yet, her eyes wrinkle at the edges when she smiles, telling me that through the brutal blows, she has also known deep and uncontrollable joy. Dave tells Marg, this is Little Dave. She needs a place to live. I step up into the porch light and Marg softens, lowering her hands from her hips, palms open. Well, Marg says, luckily for us, there's a couch in my room with no one sleeping on it. Then she says, come inside, sis, and as I step through the door, I feel so safe, perhaps safer than I've ever felt in my life, entering Uranian House, the home where I'll live for more than two decades.

I am led into the living room where I sit down on a green velvet couch. The room is an eclectic mix of mismatched furniture – a pink chaise longue beneath the wide front window, an assortment of lamps, a modern leather armchair, a Persian rug, crystal ashtrays, glasses of wine, a deck of cards spread across the coffee table in a paused game. Atop the wooden bookshelf opposite me, vines of devil's ivy flow out of pots, cascading down over the spines of the many volumes crammed onto each shelf. Paintings and prints of famous artworks and photographs are hung all around the room in clusters, so crowded that in some places, you can barely see any of the wall behind. The living room is full of things, but somehow doesn't feel cluttered. Instead, I sense the enormous amount of life that has already been lived here.

The other person from the balcony comes down the stairs and enters the living room, rolled cigarette still in hand. He's got a head of thick hair, pale cheeks and a bushy moustache, and is wearing a button-up tucked into trousers, and chunky glasses. Standing next to Johnny, who is effortlessly stylish and charismatic, this man is more reserved, quieter, introverted. Johnny tells me, this is Geoff . . . He is my boyfriend. Then the pair kiss on the lips. And I can't help but smile at this, which makes everyone else smile too.

Geoff comes and sits next to Marg and me on the couch. I introduce myself. I'm Little Dave. Geoff gives me a hug and says, it's a pleasure to meet you. Marg explains, she's going to sleep on my couch until we can organise her a room. Then she turns to Johnny and says, get me some frozen peas from the kitchen, would ya please?

Johnny comes back with frozen peas and a tea towel. Marg wraps the peas in the towel and gently holds them up to my eye. I start to tremble, and she wraps one arm around my shoulder. I let go of myself, feeling my body loosen and expand so that it takes up an impossible amount of space. And it should be awkward, becoming bigger in this way in front of strangers. But it's not. It's not awkward at all.

I yawn and Marg says, you must be exhausted. How about we take you upstairs? Dave gets up from where he's sitting on the floor and puts his hands on my shoulders. I gotta get home, he says, but you'll be okay here. He gives me a hug and says goodbye to everyone. Then, as Marg walks me up the stairs, I turn to see Johnny and Geoff consoling Dave by the front door. They're speaking in hushed voices, so quiet I can't make out the words. Marg says to me, come on. Let's get you to bed.

There's a gentle knock at the door. I slowly rouse myself and say, come in. Geoff enters, coming to sit down on the floor beside the couch. I catch my reflection in Marg's mirror. My bruised flesh is fading now from blue to yellowed brown. Geoff says, I've got something for you. He hands me a book. On the cover: *Modernism.* He says, I saw you looking at the paintings in the living room last night. I tell him, I've heard of Modernism. I was supposed to study it next term at school. He tells me, it's a fascinating history. I don't want you to miss out. Then he says, you know, I teach visual arts at a university near here. If you wanted to, we could do some lessons here at home, you and me? I open the book. It's heavy, thick with pages of glossy images, photos of contorted bodies and painted shapes. I struggle for words, so

I simply nod, feeling my eyes glass over. Many historians have attempted to erase us, Geoff says. They've never favoured those with our kind of . . . *disposition* . . . but we've always been here, in the margins . . . if you know where to look.

I turn another page and a piece of card falls out of the book. The card is handpainted, shapes of deep reds, burnt oranges, pinks, and clay whites. Geoff says, Johnny wants you to have this. His grandmother painted it . . . and it's one of only three paintings he has of hers. I hold the card up with hands that are trembling, feeling the enormous weight of this gift. Geoff tells me how he had travelled as a young art historian from Alice right up to Darwin. I was meeting artists and mistook their artworks for the kinds of abstract paintings I'd been looking at in European Modernism. But they're not abstracts . . . They're topographic maps! Geoff points to the painting in my hand. And Johnny's grandmother would have painted this to tell a story of her Country.

I confess to Geoff that I've never imagined art to be anything like this before. He smiles, neither had I. But on that trip, when I finally made it through the desert to the coast, it was the wet season and I got caught in this heavy downpour. And I ducked under the veranda of this big old pub and found Johnny standing there, back against the wall, Camel cigarette in hand, and I remember how drenched I was and how foolish I felt, and how he was completely dry and looking as gorgeous as ever. And he just laughed at me and said, you're not from 'ere, are ya? I shook my head. And then he said in a much quieter voice, next time, listen to the birds. They'll tell ya when the rain is coming. And then he offered me a Camel from his packet, and I took one, and as he lit it for me, I thought, I'm going to love this man. Geoff's glasses fog up now. He laughs and takes them off, cleaning them on his shirt. Then he says, I had been studying and writing about art for almost a decade when we met. And, well . . . Johnny changed everything for me. He's very generous with his heart.

Weeks from now, Dave will come to visit me, to see how I'm settling in. He'll bring two bottles of Coke to my new room, a room I have all to myself, and we'll sit on the wooden floor, backs against the wall, drinking our Cokes as he tells me how the day he found me, I wasn't the only one who needed saving. I'll learn that Dave loved Andrew since he was fourteen years old. That he, too, grew up in Newcastle and fucked his neighbour in the shadows of his family home. That later he married Christine and had kids and loved his wife the way he was supposed to, but that he ached for Andrew. Relentlessly. Through all the years with their almost kisses and side glances and knowing smiles, they pined in secret. And now Andrew is dead, and Dave went to the funeral with his elderly parents, and they were the 'old neighbours' from thirty years ago who sat at the back of the church because no one in that steel town knew that Dave and Andrew loved and loved and loved. Relentlessly. No one knew that Dave sat there in the church for two hours feeling like his borders had become porous and that he was spilling out through his skin. Lost to dirt and rock and ocean. Because a love that never could be, is now the love that never was.

limb two

ONE DAY ONE day one day I sit my final high school exam. It's visual arts, my second favourite subject (after English literature, of course). I fly through the paper, responding to Picasso's Cubist *Guernica*, arguing that his shattered faces and fractured limbs are a visual metaphor for wartime violence, before writing a marvellously succinct essay on Marcel Duchamp's *Fountain* and the shock of his found object, asserting that meaning is signified by context. I like to point out the irony of anti-establishment art becoming part of the Modern establishment. Thrilled with my essay, I flip the exam paper to the last question, ready to write the final paragraph of my high school education, and find myself confronted by a photo I've never seen before.

I feel a surge of panic. My pulse becomes thick in my throat. I take a deep breath and sink back through the recesses of my mind, drawing on everything I've studied in order to make sense of this work.

The caption reads, Claude Cahun, *Self-portrait*, 1927.

Claude Cahun. *French, maybe?* 1927, France. I know the artistic climate of Paris at this time, of the Surrealists, of sleep-walkers and ant eaters on leashes and warped limbs – my favourite movement of Modernism. But I've read all the readings Mrs Ballis gave us on Surrealism and nothing mentioned a Claude Cahun. Who is he? I take another breath and recall Mrs Ballis's most basic instruction . . . just tell me what you see. I look down at the photo.

In this paper reproduction, the picture is grainy, but I can imagine that the original would have been silky and rich. In the middle of the picture is Claude. His face is caked in metallic paste, shiny as a silver dish, with thin, drawn-on eyebrows and pencil-lined lips. Claude's face appears more like a mask. Beneath, his torso and legs are dressed in all black, making his body blend back and disappear into the passive black backdrop. His bare arms are painted metallic, too, but a darker pigment than that of his face. Like his arms and face belong to different bodies. I feel a kick of anxiety between my shoulders.

I look around the exam hall. My classmates hurriedly scribble their essays, seemingly unfazed, and I wonder, do they not see what I *see*?

Claude's arms bend symmetrically around a mirrored orb. The eye. I see myself reflected between Claude's bronze hands, like he is holding me inside his grasp. I feel a strange sense of exhaustion, as if the air in here is everyone else's exhalation. Like the oxygen is so sparse and far apart that I must suck in in in just to taste it.

An invigilator walks over to my desk. Would you like to step outside? she asks. Get some fresh air?

I nod and the examiner helps me to my feet. Other students are looking now. I stumble past them, all the way to the front of the hall where she glances up from her desk. Her eyes meet mine and in her panicked gaze, I come undone.

Outside, I find myself propped up against a wall. The school nurse explains to me, you're okay. You fainted, but you're okay. She hands me a cup of water. Drink this. I start to cry, sobbing hard into my palms. Because inside the hall, my exam sits unfinished. Unanswered. Open-ended –

A body casts a shadow over me. I look up and see her. You okay? she asks.

Other students are spilling from the hall. I squeeze the snot from my nose and wipe it on my school dress. She watches but doesn't flinch. I feel disgusting. I want her to look away, but she doesn't.

I didn't finish the last question, I say, my words quaking.

She kneels, touches my arm. You'll ace it anyway, she says kindly. You're the biggest nerd I know.

I look down into my lap, confessing to her, I didn't know the artist.

She laughs, tells me, none of us did! Then she lets go of my arm. You'll be fine, she says. And then she gets up and walks away.

Decades from now, I'll learn that Claude Cahun was a woman. And that Claude's life partner and collaborator, a woman named Marcel Moore, took her own life only a year before my first confrontation with Claude's portrait. That some say Marcel died to escape the pain of her arthritis. That others say she died to return to Claude, the woman with the silver face and bronze arms who held a vision of something *other* in the palms of her hands.

My mum is there with a cake and balloons. Congratulations! she says, throwing her arms around me. I collapse into her hold, as all the relief that I expected to feel emerges instead as grief. Something I cannot locate, and yet here it is, in me, feathered and metallic.

Greg arrives later. And then my dad. They shower me with their pride. With hugs and kisses, and *you're finished, hooray!*

I swallow up their words and smiles and warmth, but they spill out of me as quickly as they go in. Because this thin membrane of skin isn't enough to keep me intact.

We eat dinner together, the four of us. Greasy pork belly with stodgy rice that lumps in my stomach. I feel sick.

Oh my *God*! Mum says suddenly. I forgot the champagne!

She gets up and rushes to the fridge for the bottle. As she peels off the gold foil, her hands are shaking and there are tears in her eyes.

Are you okay? I ask, touching her arm.

Mum nods. I'm just so proud. Then she turns to Greg. I don't know if you know this, but I lost three babies, she says, choking up now. And, well, this girl right here is our little miracle! I . . . I . . .

Dad gets up from his chair and puts his arm around her.

I just never imagined I'd get to see my baby finish school, she says. It's a big day for all of us.

Then she pops the cork and they all cheer. I look at each of them and smile, squinting against the brightness of it all.

After dinner, Greg asks, should we head to the party?

I look at Mum, who is clearing the table.

Oh! Don't worry, sweet, she says, I've got this. Go! Enjoy the party! Celebrate!

Keith is hosting a graduation party. His parents are overseas, and now their house on Merewether Headland is heaving with

soon-to-be-in-the-world teenagers who are drinking cheap wine
and dancing and vomiting in pot plants and smoking joints on
the couch and fucking in the bushes. I have a bottle of sparkling
wine, which I've almost finished by the time we arrive.

Greg passes me his flask of bourbon. It scalds the insides of
my chest, but I drink more. And then I draw on his cigarette.
Breathe out hot smoke, inhale elation, because as I walk, the
ground is already moving. Rocking. Grinding back and forth.
I see her.

She is standing on the balcony that overhangs Merewether
Beach. Waves break in the darkness, emerging in silver white
wash. The horizon is entirely obscured, but I can hear the steady
crunch of water, the sweep of the tide over the blackened shore.
The night air tastes sweet. Cicadas and flower pollen and salt.

She's wearing orange flares the colour of marmalade. Her hair
is choppy ocean. I feel myself overcome by her, swallowed up
whole. Like I'm dreaming softly. It's all warm, gooey and gelatinous. Hey, I say, swimming up to her, skin tingling.

She says my name, flowers unfolding around the sound. You
okay? She holds my arm to steady me.

I nod, hiccup.

Let's get you some water, yeah?

There's the feeling of rock and roll rattling through my muscle.

There's the feeling of her hands in my hair, holding it back as
vomit surges from my throat.

There's my coughing that feels like skin ripping.

There's the feeling of my belly clenching as I gag on the nothing that's left.

There's the feeling of her palm rubbing the flat between my shoulder blades.

There's the feeling of my head lolling back, my eyeballs rolling around like loose marbles.

There's the feeling of words spilling from my mouth. Out out out they come. Gushing over my lips. Pooling in her lap.

There's the sound of her voice in my ear, *shhh*.

I open my eyes and I'm in a car. Greg is beside me in the driver's seat, fists clenched around the wheel. Your dad is gonna kill me when he sees how fucking pissed you are! He's slurring his words. Greg presses his foot heavy on the accelerator. He reeks of bourbon. Or I do. Or we both do. I wind down my window. My hair whips against my face, stinging sharp at the ends where it's matted with dried vomit. Greg throws the car around a corner. I am sobering up with each surge of fear.
Slow down, I say. Please!
Fuck you.

I wake and a blur of shadow takes the shape of a woman. Mum comes into focus. She lets go of a giant breath and bursts into tears. Oh, honey! Thank God, thank *God*!
My eyelids are thick clouds, pressing down.

When I open them again, the light has changed. It's bright sunshine. I squint. She's there, holding my hand. Dad is here too.

You're okay, kiddo, he says, smiling through watery, bloodshot eyes. You're in a hospital. There was an accident. But you're going to be okay.

I open my mouth to ask, what happened? But nothing moves, only pain, surging through my jawbone, sharp, splitting my temples.

Mum tells me my jaw is broken, that I'm missing three teeth, that they've realigned my jaw. But don't you worry, she says, gently holding my hand. They're going to replace them when your bones have healed.

With every word she utters, I become more aware of my flesh, swollen smooth and bulging. I slip the tip of my tongue into the gummy holes where my front teeth should be. I feel my eyes begin to water, overwhelmed by the shock of it all.

There's a window on the other side of the room, and I catch my reflection in the glass. A swarm of goosebumps spreads across my skin, and my mouth fills with bloody water, my breath growing sharp with grief. My face is a gory mess of bruises and wire. I look desperately at myself, hoping to recognise something in those eyes that will connect this face to the body I know. But the neck of distance between is irreparably long.

Mum tells me, Greg is okay.

Dad grunts and says that he'd be better off dead.

Then she leans in and tells me that I won't be seeing Greg anymore, that he's not my boyfriend now. She says, we've spoken to his parents, and this is what we've all decided.

I feel her words moving through my body. And it surprises me that this ending doesn't snag. There's no pinching of muscle, no wool caught in the nettle. Her words just sail through, like air, in and out. Painlessly. Just like that, Greg and I are over.

I know this must be hard to hear, Mum says, but he almost killed you. And, well, we believe this is for the best, and I hope you'll see that soon. And anyway, she says, reaching down into her bag, we have something we think will make you very happy. Mum pulls an envelope out and draws a letter from it. She reads it aloud: Congratulations. You have been offered an early place in our English Literature program. Should you accept, your Bachelor will be supported by a generous scholarship. Mum throws the piece of paper up in the air. Her joy is bursting, bright pink.

Dad kisses the top of my head. We're so proud of you.

And anyway, Mum says, there'll be lots of lovely boys for you to meet when you get to university. For now, let's just focus on getting you all fixed up.

Here I am, witnessing my future go from dreamt to real, like dusk dissolving pink so that all the stars finally become visible. The whole of the universe suddenly before me, infinitely detailed and possible.

Wow.

There's a knock at the door and she appears. I swallow rust. Mum kisses my hands and taps my dad on the shoulder. Come on, she says, let's go get a coffee.

I close my eyes, try to steady my breath. When I open them, she is pulling up a chair beside my bed. She notices the letter on the floor, picks it up, scans the text. Whoa, she says, that's great. Though not surprising. Told you you'd be fine. Then she looks down into her lap. Starts playing with her grandmother's ring. I notice her hands are shaking. And it's like someone has punctured my lungs with a metal pick, because I'm holding my breath, but all the air is escaping.

Finally, she says, I don't know how much you remember from the other night . . . You said some things. I . . . I don't think I should repeat them. But I guess I know now why you did what you did . . . with Greg and everything. I know you didn't really want him. You wanted . . .

She doesn't finish the sentence. She can't bring herself to.

The machine that is monitoring my pulse begins to beep faster and faster.

She watches my pulse race green across the screen and I feel horrifically exposed. I want to tell her that it's not true, that she's wrong about me. That I loved Greg and she doesn't have to worry. That she doesn't have to leave me. Please don't leave me. But my mouth is wired shut.

I want to tell her that it's all true, that she's right about me. That I never loved Greg, and this was all for her. But that it's okay. This is okay. We'll survive. Please, please don't leave me. But my mouth is wired shut.

She looks me deep in the eye. I don't want this. I never have. And I never will, okay? I'll never want you like that.

A moment passes, and then a sound comes out of me from somewhere deep down. It's primal, this wailing. Shocking, even to me. I desperately want to shut myself up. But this guttural cry rises up and out of me, beyond my control. The body takes over, like I am animal, undead, haunted. Humiliated. My parents rush in with a nurse who asks me questions I cannot hear, her words drowned out by the roar of the pain in me, feral, clawing from the inside out.

More nurses hurry in, pushing my parents out of the way. It's chaos, all wings flapping and feathers flying.

She is backed against a wall, watching me. She edges towards the door. Slips out. Out of my life. Gone. And I know already that I will never see her again, not in the flesh of the awake. Only in dreams, where she will lurk in the river veins of my limbs, stirring from time to time like silt stirred up from the bed of my sleeping body, clouding the water. And I will wake every time in the cold sweat of this very heartbreak, as if no time has passed at all. Because the river of mountain memory is achingly fresh. And my face will be wet with tears, not because I've dreamt of her again after all these years, but because in this dream, I am kissing her, and now I've woken up.

limb one

MARG COMES INTO my room and rips open the blinds. I wince at the suddenness of afternoon light. You'll be late to work, she says. Again. *Thanks, Mum*, I joke, and Marg rolls her eyes, leaving my room as abruptly as she entered.

I turn over and sling my arms around her shoulders, gently pulling her naked body against mine, smiling. I kiss her. We stink of cum and sweat and last night's beers. That was fun, I whisper. She asks, will I see you again? Sure, I reply, I'll be around. I hold her hand down the hallway, kiss her goodbye at the door. Closing it behind her, I rub sleep from my eyes. Geoff is sitting in the living room, drawing on his liquorice-papered cigarette. Who was that? he asks. I shrug and he laughs and says, more lovers than years around the sun.

I make coffee with Johnny in the kitchen. Mine is strong, black, no sugar. He puts powdered milk in his, stirring vigorously until the powder has entirely dissolved. It's almost five, he says, and chucks me the keys to the bar. I'll be there around seven. Who's performing tonight? I ask. Open mic, he says, don't you read the schedule? I like surprises, I smirk, keeps things interesting. Yeah, yeah, well you're supposed to be helping Daphne set up, so would be good if ya paid attention to what day of the week it was. I laugh, kiss him on the cheek, then bolt up the stairs, singing over my shoulder, love you too!

I walk through the streets I love, my tank tucked into green slacks. I know this inner-city enclave now like the back of my hand. The maze of alleyways, the rise and fall of each road, the bars and the clubs and the beats. The places to avoid, the parks to sprint through. The smells of oil and damp brick, sweat and cabbage palm, garbage and tobacco, exhaust smoke and fig, engulfing me like a homecoming.

The late sun slants between buildings. Shadows are pricked with the chill of early autumn. Up ahead, three men sit at the kerb at the back of a restaurant. Silhouettes chaining cigs. They are beefy bodies with beers in hand. I casually cross to the other side of the road, hands in pockets. As I pass them, I feel their eyes pointed at my body, my short mop of hair, my clenched jaw. One of them whistles; I look over my shoulder. He shouts, not you, *dyke*! And the shadows fill with laughter. Automatically, I give them the finger, and it's not until he jumps to his feet that I see my hand outstretched in front of me. *Oh shit*, I mutter, and then I am running. He chases, but he is slow and heavy, footsteps thudding, and I am lightning fast. When I make it to Oxford Street, I glance back and see that the prick is long gone, given up. Good riddance.

I unlock the blue door, descend the stairs into my second home and begin setting up the bar. But first, I pour myself a shot of Jack Daniel's. The drink goes down hot in my throat. Daphne enters the bar and tells me to save some for the customers. Breakfast of champions! I whip back. My God, she says, the tongue on you. I laugh and pour her a shot. She shakes her head, says, no thanks, love. So, I drink hers too.

Daphne and Johnny take turns on the mic between each act. Daphne struts across the stage with her big, vivacious energy, theatrically throwing her hair back, hyping the crowd. *Oh, come on. I can't hear you! Tell me again, how are we tonight?* Then Johnny jumps up, long legs and lean muscle, in his tight black pants, leather belt and tucked-in singlet, slicked hair and gold earring, all radiant and glamorous. He gets everyone laughing with his cheeky banter. *Things get better with age . . . Can't you tell, Daphne? I'm approaching magnificent!* Daphne does a twirl on the spot. Throws one arm up in the air, strikes a pose. *Look at me! I've already arrived!*

Greta and Sam, who've just smoked a joint outside and are already several beers deep, stumble up on stage to sing a duet. Dave is sitting on a stool at the bar. He turns to me while I'm drying glasses and says, oh here we go. I laugh and reply, better strap in! Daphne passes Sam and Greta their mics and Johnny hits play on Roberta Flack's 'Killing Me Softly'. By the time they reach the chorus, Dave and I are in stitches, laughing so hard our cheeks hurt, blocking our ears with our fingers. Jesus Christ, Dave says, they really are killing us softly with this song! Then Sam, who is wearing a blonde wig, takes off the wig and throws it at the audience in the final chorus, his bald head shining pink with sweat. He says, fuck me, it's hot up here! Then burps, which makes Greta crack up laughing, so hard she can't finish the song. It's a total shitshow of a performance, and yet, as the music fades out, we yahoo and clap just the same, cheering on our friends with our whole hearts.

When Tony, to our surprise, throws down a shot of tequila and says, right, okay, my turn! Dave and I look at each other, wide-eyed, unsure of what to expect. Dave asks me, you heard Tony sing before? I shake my head. No, never. Tony's hands are trembling when he takes the mic, but as King Harvest's 'Dancing in the Moonlight' begins to belt through the bar, Tony's hips sway in time with the beat, and we see his nerves settle. As he opens with the first line, Dave says to me, bloody hell, he's actually quite good! I nod, yeah, wow. Who knew? I pick up another glass from the sink and begin towelling it dry, my gaze settling on Dave, who is looking at Tony with a reverence I've never seen in him before. I watch him watching Tony until the song finishes and Dave stands up and joins the crowd for a standing ovation. Tony does a bow, then jumps off the stage and comes back to the bar. Dave tries to speak, but his words are all over the place. He's completely flustered. I laugh. Spit it out, mate! He laughs, too, says, shut up, Little Dave! Then he looks to Tony, blushing. Wow, Dave says. Tony grins. And I smile to myself, sensing somewhere deep down that I am witnessing a small, but glorious beginning.

Marg comes into the bar late with Geoff, her arm slung around his shoulder. His face is sullen, shoulders slouched. Hers is tight with rage. What's going on? I ask her as I crack open a beer and pass it to her. They've fired Geoff, she says, then takes a swig of her beer, downing half the bottle in one giant gulp. They did *what*? exclaims Daphne, cheeks flushed. Johnny, who is standing beside me, rounds the bar and takes Geoff in his arms. He whispers something in his ear, and I watch Geoff come apart. Johnny catches Geoff's slow tears, wiping them away with his gentle touch. Bastards! Marg says, throwing down the rest of her beer. Thinking they're *so* smart! But they're not, Johnny says. The universities are just as bad as all the rest.

Back home, in our living room, people have gathered. There is talk of a protest. Tomorrow. We'll show them! Fucking dogs! Marg says, striding back and forth. Everyone is talking logistics, arguing over the top of each other. But what's our goal? Marg asks. We're getting him his job back, Johnny snaps, as if that part is obvious. He can't go back to working there, says Sam. Sure he can, says Tony. That's bullshit. – What would you know? You don't know these people. – They're fucked, the lot of them. – Don't be so existential. – Fuck off. – I'm just realistic . . . Sorry that you're floating around in la la land! – I just think the aim isn't to reinstate him. – Well, what do you want then? – We need to show that the university is fucked. – *Of course* it's fucked, that's the whole point. – Exactly! – No! Not exactly! – We need direction, protests don't mean anything if we don't have a goal. – Well, what's our goal? – Oh, for crying out loud!

While they all storm about and argue, Geoff and I share a cigarette. We are sitting on the floor, backs against the wall, legs outstretched on the rug I found last year discarded in an alleyway at the back of the Cross. He passes the rollie to me. I smile. He tries to smile back, but his lips are trembling. I feel so small, he says. I hold his hand. He takes back the rollie. Draws on it. Blows smoke silently so that it plumes between us. The cloud stings my eyes and I laugh, fanning it away from my face. He chuckles and I think, thank God, his smile . . . there it is. I kiss Geoff's knuckles. You'll survive, I say. Because what else is there? Geoff purses his lips. You're secretly a wise old soul, he says, just trapped in this young person's body, aren't you? I smirk. Not really, I stole that one from Daphne. Geoff giggles and his joy fans from the belly outwards in wide shakes. Ah, yes, well . . . the best poets steal. I ask him, did you steal that? He nods. I kiss him on the cheek. Love you, Geoff. I love you, too, Little Dave.

Marg comes into my room and is surprised to find me awake, dressed, blinds open. She asks me, are you okay? I laugh out loud. You have such low expectations of me! She shakes her head. I'm just surprised, she says. I tell her that I wouldn't miss today for the world, that this is my family. She smiles and kisses me on the forehead. Yep, we are. Then she grabs me by the hand and says, come on, let's go.

On the train and in the streets, we are a spectacle. Our bodies are a photomontage of unlikely images, assembled so artfully we create a brilliant new picture, stuck together with glue and staples. We are united. Neither their pointed eyes nor pointed fingers can tear this picture apart, because we are bolstered by our rage and our love. Because when you humiliate and make small, the rest of us become bigger to fill the space, holding the family portrait intact.

Outside the university gates, we gather. CAMP members, student unionists, friends from the bar, the whole of Uranian House. I look up at the gates, old and ornate, the university beyond a physical clash of architectures. Concrete, sandstone, glass, sprawling lawns and ripe trees. I've never been here before, at least not in the flesh of the awake. Only in daydreams, when I sat alone in the library all those years ago thinking one day one day one day, I'll study here. Now here I am, shaggy haired, in a woollen jumper and denim jeans, with big sunglasses and strong arms, carrying a placard that reads,

I

AM

LESBIAN

AND

I AM

BEAUTIFUL

On the way here, Johnny told me, only half joking, that my sign was all about me and nothing to do with Geoff or his reinstatement. To which I rebutted, well, it's the truth. And Daphne snort laughed.

I come alive amid this hum of bodies; my limbs are vibrating gold. Everything is charged and electric. There must be close to thirty people here. I marvel at the immensity of our success, of our coming together at such short notice. The thrill of it all surges through us. Makes our cries full-throated, drowning out the air. We chant and scream and sing, moving through the campus like a murmuration, bending, expanding, contracting when the police appear.

We rush to bring Daphne into the centre of our group, to hold her in the heart, because we know all too well the sickening glee these pigs feel when they steal our matriarchs.

Stop police attacks!
On gays, women and Blacks!

The cops begin to pick us off at the edges, ripping limbs from the body. That's when I see her.

She doesn't look remarkable. She is wearing a casual black t-shirt and faded black jeans. Her blood orange hair is pulled tight. Amid the devolving chaos and the tearing of limbs, she thrusts a sign into the sky that reads,

I

AM

A

SEXUAL

BEING

And it's not that she looks particularly striking. Yet I am entirely struck by her, like lightning into sand, transforming my body into glass, so that I suddenly become translucent and utterly breakable. Because she carries herself in a way that I've never witnessed in anyone before. As if she is breaking apart in the same moment that she is becoming whole, both coming undone and being built through the violence of metamorphosis – the process of taking shape. I feel I am in there, watching this clash of opposites. Because she is as terrified as she is defiant.

A sexual being, I think, full of pleasure and pain. For reasons I don't understand but feel, I want to be closer to her.

I grab Geoff's arm. Point through the crowd of people and placards to her. Geoff, I say, who is that? *What?* he asks. That woman, do you know her? He gives me a look as if to say, you *cannot* be serious. Suddenly a policeman takes hold of my jumper, pulls me backwards. I trip and fall to the ground, landing hard on my arse. In the fall, the policeman loses his grip on me. I reach for Geoff's hand, and he yanks me to my feet. And then we are running, along with everyone else. Fleeing the university grounds in every direction so that it's impossible for the police to catch all of us.

Geoff and I make it out through the gates and round a corner where we run into Johnny. You two okay? he asks, panting heavily. Geoff tells him we're fine, but that the cops got several people. Johnny says he'll go with CAMP to the station, then notices my elbow is bleeding. You two should go home, he says, get fixed up. I'll meet you back there later. He kisses the top of Geoff's hand and then he is off.

We duck into a pub and sneak into the bathrooms together. Geoff helps me wash my arm clean. So, do you know who she was? I ask. Geoff is confused. Who? That woman, I explain, the one with the sign that said, I am a sexual being. He lets slip an exasperated laugh. Our friends just got arrested, and all you can think about is your next lay? I shrug. I'm selfish . . . water is wet. Are you surprised? He chuckles, says, no, I guess not. I look at

Geoff with pleading eyes, make prayer hands. Fine, he says at last. Caragh. Her name is Caragh. She took one of my classes last term. So she's an artist? She's studying fine art, yes. I grin, he shakes his head. You're unbelievable.

limb two

BREAKFAST IS SERVED in a hall of portraits. Every day begins this way. Two fried eggs, a slice of burnt toast, a spurt of tomato sauce, a watery sausage. Scoffed down beneath the crusty gazes of painted white men who pose with their accolades and their riches. There is talk at the long table this morning of the Ashes. I chime in when they begin talking about the new Gray-Nicolls scoop. I'd love to see The Don play with it, I say.

Well, you can't, Scott snaps. He's retired.

Thank you, I say, Captain Obvious.

Scott snorts. What would *you* know about cricket anyway?

I got really into it one summer.

He rolls his eyes.

Seriously! I was in hospital, and it was all that was on the ra—

Why were you in hospital? Robert asks, talking over the top of me.

I broke my jaw in a car accident. See these? I say, tapping my finger against my two front teeth. Fake!

Robert exclaims, Whoa! No kidding, they look so real. He reaches out and touches my tooth.

Scott's face twists with disgust. Gross! he says.

I push Robert's hand away and close my mouth.

I sound different these days. When I go home at Christmas, everyone tells me how smart I sound. And I resent them for it, because when I start term again in February, I must work extra hard to clean the coal off my accent.

I meet Jen at the beginning of second year when she asks to borrow a pen for our elective in Nature Writing. It feels like a wonderful cliché, because I am *that* student. The one with ample blue pens, highlighters and pencils. Paper tabs to flag important sections of text.

Why did you pick this class? she asks.

I love Judith Wright, I tell her. What about you?

Because I looked at the reading list, and it's all European men . . . I guess I'm curious.

I love my university, the clash of architectures. Grand old sandstone. Spindly spires. Brutalist concrete blocks. Panes of tinted glass. Sprawling grasses and trees that bow. I love the sounds of shoes on pavement, chatter in the hallways – did you finish your paper? What are you reading? I love the cool silences of the library, hushed voices, whispering, want to get a coffee? Everything is big ideas and bright conversation, picked at and teased apart. Learning, I realise, is a process of untangling.

Walking out of our final Nature Writing class, Jen asks me, what did you think of today?

I loved it! Especially what he was saying about the splitting of culture and nature in the English language during the Enlightenment, and how defining the two as opposites has shaped the way we think about nature, even to this day . . . What did you think?

I mean, it's all very Eurocentric, but I guess that's hardly surprising. Do you have any idea what you want to write your essay about? I can't believe it's due so soon!

I tell Jen I'm writing mine on Annie Dillard's *Pilgrim at Tinker Creek*. I'm going to argue that she exploited the tropes of nature writing to situate herself within a male-dominated genre, only to subvert it from the inside out.

Jen makes a face. Male dominated, sure . . . but also very white.

Yeah, I say, but we're both white, so like, shouldn't we write–

Jen cuts me off. I'm not white, she says.

I stop beside her and feel myself frowning. I look at her, confused. What do you mean?

I mean that I might pass as white to you, she says. But that's because this colony has made a concerted effort since invasion to eradicate my people.

Oh, I say. Sorry, Jen. I honestly didn't think . . .

She shrugs. We're studying 'nature' writing, perhaps you should think about what a European white man's nature writing really means here.

I open the door for us, but before I can gather my thoughts to respond, the sound of distant screaming rushes in, haunting the hall. Can you hear that? I ask.

Yeah. Let's check it out.

Nerves prick the underside of my flesh. We walk out of the hallway, round the corner of the building, and the ominous screams take the shape of chants.

Stop police attacks!
On gays, women and Blacks!

I notice a girl I've seen before. Around the humanities, maybe art, maybe history. She's a student, like me. Wearing a casual t-shirt and faded jeans, hair pulled tight, like me. She is like me, like me, like me. Thrusting a sign into the sky that reads,

I

AM

A

SEXUAL

BEING

She is *un*like me.

Jen begins muttering the chant as if she already knows it, as if she's been here before. And maybe she has. Because now she is shouting. She grabs my hand and pulls me into the crowd.

The protesters are mostly my age, though a few are older. One woman, wearing a t-shirt printed with the image of a clenched fist, leads the chant through a megaphone. Suddenly, she flicks on the siren. I turn and see police swarming.

I begin to run. Maybe Jen sees me run. Maybe she thinks, *coward.*

My body collides with another. We fall to the ground, winded on concrete. Someone shouts, *Daphne!* And then a hand with purple-painted nails reaches down. A rush of pink satin. The hand grips *my* hand. Brown skin. Smooth and cool. I feel myself recoil, pulling back.

He looks down at me. There is hurt in his eyes.

The friend says, *Johnny! Let's go!*

He takes another look at me lying on the ground. The sun behind him makes his ears shine pink, a fleshy halo of second chances, and he looks at me as if he recognises something in my body. He reaches, grabs my hand again and this time I let him. He hoists me to my feet. This man's voice is pressing as he says, come on, this way!

And in this moment, I *could* follow. This moment . . . passed. Because a police officer grabs me by the arm and yanks me backwards. I turn and lift my hands up, panic surging. Shout, I'm just a student! Please! I'm a student.

The officer's aggression suddenly loosens. Are you okay?

I nod, straightening my skirt. Hands trembling.

Did you see where they went?

That way, I say as I point down between two buildings. They went that way.

I watch the police officer race down the alleyway, to a future I may never know. Because a voice says,

Hey.

I turn around and see a young man holding a stack of books.

You're bleeding, he says, pointing.

I look down at my elbow, at the small bulbs of blood.

Here, he says, drawing a handkerchief from his pocket. I take it and dab the graze. I'm Thomas, he says. I offer him back the handkerchief and he laughs, softly, small creases at the edges of his smile. You can keep it.

Oh . . . yeah, I say. Thanks.

You're welcome.

He's handsome, in an unassuming way. He doesn't have dimples, or a striking jawline, or muscular arms. But he carries himself with a quiet confidence, a kind tenderness. Hair brushed to one side. A thin silver chain around his neck. A soft smile around the eyes.

I grin and tell him my name.

We shake hands. Can I get you something? Water? A coffee? How about a beer?

He grins. I know a good pub just down the road.

Thomas speaks the way feathers fall. In that roundabout way where the words drift and ebb and are slow to land. Still, I listen, as he tells me what he's reading, what he's writing. And it isn't that he's particularly charming, yet I am entirely charmed by him. He meanders in a way that is open and inviting, like wandering into a forest, smile spreading, saying, I'm not sure where I'm going, but would you like to walk with me?

We swap books and I learn him in the margins. I learn him in the words he's underlined and the pages he's folded. Sometimes, I read a passage and find he's written at the edge everything I want to say, as though he has lifted the thought straight out of my heart. I lie awake at night, beneath the glow of my lamp, poring over the pages, touching where he's spilt coffee, the ink smudged, lifting the book to smell his skin. I lightly touch my mouth to the paper, feeling the coarseness of it against my lips. Learning him is a quiet and slow undertaking.

And I am taken.

Breakfast is served in a hall of portraits, as every day begins. Two fried eggs, a slice of burnt toast, a spurt of tomato sauce, a watery sausage. Scoffed down beneath the crusty gaze of painted white men who pose with their accolades and their riches. There is talk at the long table this morning of the end-of-term winter social. Robert says he's taking Leanne, which comes as a surprise to Leanne.

She scoffs and says, in your dreams, but before the laughter dies down, she reaches across and touches Robert's hand, quietly grins, saying, yeah, I mean, *obviously*.

Scott asks me, what about you?

I shrug, tell him, I know someone I can ask.

My hand is resting on Thomas's copy of *Metamorphoses*. I press my thumb against its tender spine. He spots me and walks over. Can I sit down? I nod and he pulls up a chair at the desk beside me. The air in the library is neither hot nor cold, benign in a way that makes this shiver of goosebumps feel all the more magical. My skin feels like it's sparkling. I finished *Pilgrim at Tinker Creek*, he whispers, and your essay. He smiles, then says, I think it's brilliant.

And I think I might crack open, or that I *am* cracking open, because of the way he responds to all the points I was most proud of, praising my writing, the clarity and the insight. I am blushing, but I'm not embarrassed, because he is blushing too.

I think, he says, that you are brilliant.

And I already want to follow him, into the forest, wherever he wants to go. I want to wander and meander with him. I want to take time, to be together slowly, because I want this bloom to last forever.

Thomas, I whisper, I'd quite like to kiss you.

He giggles, looks over his shoulder, around, as if checking that there's no one else, that I am, indeed, talking to him. He leans forward. I lean forward. He grins, and so do I, because I thought

I needed to be something else. That I needed to transform in order to realise. But here I am. All along, here I was, right here, waiting. That sullen branch you thought was dead. Here is spring, opening and unfolding. In a building full of books, we kiss, and words cascade over shelves. This is how I will tell the story. Because in this moment, I feel already the grand beginning of everything beyond. It swells my body like I am rolling clouds, like I am wood submerged in river water.

This is how I will tell the story of falling in love with a novelist before he became one.

limb one

It surprises me that no one checks me at the door. I file into the auditorium with all the other students and imagine, for a moment, another story playing out. One where I remain living my first life. Swimming in the silent dark and losing my virginity in the sand dunes. Like all the other kids. One where I finish school and get a letter, saying, congratulations, you've won! We'd love to have you. Please, come, join us! One where I am living here, on campus, eating in the hall of a prestigious college, waltzing around like I fucking own the place. Whispering in the library to friends I've made, saying, want to get a coffee? One where I see her, sitting in the front row, and walk up to her and ask, politely, can I sit beside you? But this is not that story.

I sit at the back of the auditorium in the shadows and avoid eye contact. Waiting. Caragh is the last student to enter. I follow her body, weaving between students who have gathered on the stairs. I sense her rushed excitement, her purpose. She kisses a friend on the cheek. He has saved her a seat in the front row. They sit down and begin chatting. I'm too far away to hear what she's saying, but I watch how she animates the story with her hands. I think, maybe I could get closer . . . then the professor walks in, and everyone assumes their seats. He stands behind the lectern and the chatter is hushed. Above him, an image is projected onto a giant screen. It's an image I've never seen before. A man, I think, in black and white, wearing a chequered jacket, collar up high around the neck. He's standing chest to a mirror, hand gripping the top button. His gaze is doubled, because in the moment he looks to the camera his reflection looks *elsewhere*. I do a double take. A man? Or a *woman*? The thought makes my skin dance.

This, the professor says, is Claude Cahun. I sit at the back of the auditorium, utterly transfixed as the professor picks at and teases apart the image. I realise, learning is a process of untangling. Because he tugs on a string and the tight fabric of everything I thought I knew unravels. *Seeing* Claude is an undoing.

I wish I'd brought a pen, because all these words are rushing through me so fast and I feel the greatest sense of spine-tingling urgency to hold on to them all. Perhaps this is how they all feel, every time they sit in a class, getting their hearts cracked open. How lucky I feel to be in here, experiencing this great unravelling. I look around and notice a guy with his head slumped in his hand and want to shake the shit out of him. Wake up! Don't you get it? Don't you *understand*? Look at where you are!

Any questions? asks the professor. Caragh is first to stick up her hand. He sighs, as if he already knows to brace himself. I hold my breath, hot with anticipation. You've spoken a lot about Claude's work in concert with Breton and Desnos and Bataille, but you haven't, not even once, mentioned Marcel Moore. Why is that? she asks fervently. Because Moore is irrelevant to the specifics of this discussion, the professor dryly says. Caragh, without missing a beat, rebuts, irrelevant? Yes, he repeats, *irrelevant*. Caragh scoffs, then says, but everything they made, they made together! I know *that*, he says, getting frustrated now, but this seminar is on Claude's work in isolation. Caragh fires back, how can you look at her work in 'isolation' when it is always intimately bound with Marcel's? The professor lays his hand on the lectern, as if squashing the discussion beneath his palm. I'm moving on, he says. Any other questions? *Maybe,* Caragh says, you don't want to admit— He cuts her off. I said, I'm moving on. Caragh continues anyway – that they were *lesbians*! Someone in the middle row gasps. Murmurs sweep through the auditorium. The professor's face is shiny red. He asks her to leave, though it's not really a question. And as she packs up her notebook, I realise I am still holding my breath.

I feel as if my lungs are on fire, like I might, in a moment, smell the reek of my muscle burning. I exhale as she storms up the stairs and will her to look at me – *look at me*. I lean forward, out of the shadows and into the light. She glances sideways. Beneath the gaze of Claude Cahun, our eyes meet. She pauses, a flinch of confusion, like she *almost* recognises me. Or at least, this is how I will tell the story. Because in this moment, I feel already the grand beginning of everything beyond. It swells my body like I am rolling clouds, like I am wood submerged in river water. I smile. And then she is gone.

The university breaks for term and I endure the winter. I spend my nights downstairs in the bar, scanning the crowd of familiar faces for hers. Some days, I dream of Caragh. And then I wake in my room and immediately squeeze my eyes shut, hoping to re-enter the dream, but it never works. I just lie there, alone, with it all unfinished. One day, I touch myself, and imagine her, reaching up inside me, turning me inside out so that pain and pleasure intertwine.

I buy a journal. The paper is nonlined, and smooth like buttermilk. I open the cover and write.

I

AM

A

SEXUAL

BEING

Johnny asks me if I'm doing okay. Yeah, I say, exhaling a mouthful of smoke by the back door, why? Marg passes me a mug of coffee, says, we just noticed it's been a while. I ask, since what? Though I can already guess. Johnny says, since we've been woken up by you fucking someone. Ha! laughs Marg. I wasn't gonna put it that bluntly. I'm celibate now, I tell them. Johnny frowns. You sure you're . . . okay? I'm *fine,* I'm just saving myself. Marg snorts, for who? The Virgin Mary? Actually . . . I say, sipping my coffee between puffs of my cigarette, her name is Caragh. Geoff is in the courtyard hanging out his washing. I see him smiling. Marg asks, who's Caragh? To which Geoff responds, she was one of my students. I boast, she's an artist. Geoff smirks. Have you even seen her art? No, I say. He laughs, then takes my cigarette, draws and exhales. Yes, well she's very talented. I can give you that much. I grin. Oh, come on, tell me more!

Spring flowers across the university lawns and I sneak back into the arts department, one week, and then another, before I pipe up the courage to ask another student, where is Caragh? Oh, he says, I haven't seen her this term. Another girl overhears and chimes in, I'm pretty sure she dropped out.

She never comes to the house. Or to the bar. I never run into her on the sidewalk of Oxford Street. Or on the sand at Lady Bay, where summer languishes blue and green. And so, I am left, feverishly remembering, until her face is a memory of a memory of a memory of a memory, like ink in water, dispersing, and I'm not sure if we ever locked eyes at all.

We throw a dinner party for Geoff's birthday. It's late summer and the evening is balmy and pale blue. I hang a string of lights in the vines over the courtyard and lay a red and white checkered cloth across the table. I wedge pink candlesticks in empty wine bottles and set them between vases of flannel flowers. Johnny has been in the kitchen making bully beef with steamed rice. Uranian House smells of garlic and soy sauce, onion and Keens curry powder. Inside, I help Sam dice tomatoes and pile them into a porcelain dish in the shape of an open clam. We drizzle the tomatoes with olive oil until they're shining, then season with salt and pepper, and garnish with basil from the garden. I reach in to steal a piece and Sam swats my hand away. Then he steals one himself, shoving it in his mouth. Hey! I shriek. I saw that! Daphne comes in and uncorks the wine. The kitchen is crowded and alive.

I roll a cigarette and light it in the doorway. Marg asks for a drag, then walks away with it, so I roll another. Johnny pulls his pot of stew off the heat. Geoff leans over his shoulder and says, it smells delicious! Johnny is beaming. Only the best for you, he says. One day, Geoff says as he kisses the nape of Johnny's neck, I'm going to marry you. And I feel the throb of this moment. Because, against the impossibility of it all, joy persists.

We drink and eat in the open air, laughing in gusts so hard half the candles get blown out. We raise our glasses beneath the twinkling fairy lights. To Geoff! And in this paper-thin pocket of glorious now, I think, we could be *anywhere*. As if, beyond our passionfruit vines, a rocky cliff might descend all the way down to a sparkling Mediterranean Sea. Thank you, says Geoff with glassy eyes. I just love you all *so* much. I look around the table of fifteen, at my friends shoulder to shoulder, the candle wax dripping and cigarette ash burning holes in the tablecloth. Red-wine lips grinning, everyone singing. I think, look at us. *Witness us.* In a world that wishes for our annihilation, here are our bodies, spectacularly colliding.

See! yells Johnny, coming into the kitchen, where Marg and I are sitting on the benchtop. This is what I'm talking about! Marg takes a puff on Johnny's cigar, resting her head against mine. She blows out a mouthful of smoke and says over the music beating out of the living room, what you on about? He throws his hands wide. This! He climbs up onto the kitchen bench and sits down beside us, grinning. We keep protesting and all people see is our rage, but I want them to see *this*! Marg and I exchange glances. Johnny is drunk and slurring his words, but his excitement is spreading all around us. Look! he says, pointing to the living room where more friends are spilling in through the front door, shedding layers and softening with relief, as if to say, here I am, I'm home! Johnny grins at the friends dancing half naked on the table, at the lovers making out against the wall, at the spilt wine and discarded clothes. This is what I'm talking about! *Our JOY!* I'm sick of the world seeing me as this angry Black man *and* a sinning homosexual! It's killing me, Marg! She yells over the music, we're mad for good reason! I know, I know, says Johnny, but look at our family. Look at our joy, our glorious, glorious joy. It's fucking radiating and all I want is for the world to see that I am bursting in love! Johnny points down the hallway to Geoff, who is dancing with Dave and Tony. I love that man. And he loves me! Can you believe it? He doesn't exoticise me. And he isn't trying to turn me into something I'm not. He just loves me! *All* of me! Johnny kisses Marg wet on the mouth, and then me, and I don't know who is more shocked, but we both crack up laughing. Geoff dances into the kitchen and Johnny jumps down off the bench, throws his arms around his boyfriend, and sings out, I want the whole goddamn world to know that I LOVE GEOFF BLOOM!

limb two

THE NIGHT AIR is fresh, black and biting. We hurry from the common room across the quad to the hall where they're holding a winter social dance. I'm wearing a fancy satin dress that swooshes and sways, which my mum borrowed off her friend. Beneath, I have pale pink stockings and sparkly shoes. Thomas says, you look beautiful.

I laugh and say, I feel ridiculous!

Thomas is wearing a tuxedo and has his hair combed back. He looks dashingly handsome, but I can't bring myself to tell him that, worried it'll come out all gushy and weird, so I just say, don't you scrub up okay!

Inside the hall, there's an ice sculpture of a dolphin, surrounded by flutes of champagne. The walls are decorated with snow-flakes cut out of iridescent cardboard and there's an extravagant candelabra with blue beeswax candles burning at the centre of every table.

When the senior professors file in, we all stand. Then, as they take their seats on their high table at the front of the hall, we are invited to be seated.

Waiters begin setting down plates of food. We are served roast chicken with glistening gravy, duck-fat fried potatoes and caramelised baby carrots. For dessert, we are given sticky date pudding with vanilla ice cream and generous pours of caramel sauce. All of it is washed down with a seemingly endless supply of champagne and red wine.

We're standing out the front of a pub on King Street when Scott puts down the flute of champagne he stole from our table and pulls a packet of cigarettes from his jacket pocket. It's an obscene display of wealth, he says as he lights a tailor Marlboro. He passes the packet to Thomas and Thomas takes one, then lights it.

Thomas blows out smoke, turns to me and says, Scott *calls* himself a communist.

Scott frowns and says, Marxist, actually.

Thomas says, if you had such a problem with the obscene display of wealth, why did you buy a ticket?

Everyone should be entitled to a good party, he says as he takes another drag of his cigarette.

Thomas laughs, then shuts his mouth when it becomes obvious that Scott isn't joking.

Across the street, three women in sparkling dresses and towering heels strut down the sidewalk. As they get closer, a guy at the table beside us yells at them, Oi! *OI!!!!*

The women huddle together, quickening their pace towards the city.

The guy turns back to his table and remarks, fucking *feral*.

When I look back at Thomas and Scott, they are both laughing.

limb one

THEY SAY THEY'RE going to call it Mardi Gras.

'Mardi Gras'

I know this name from
Sundays, life past. It meant,
Fat Tuesday,
fill me up. It meant,
pancakes and syrup. Fill me up,
filled up.

Now it's Mardi Gras,
today, it's us, but with
all the connotations,

                                        lingering . . .

Because the past promise of fatness and fullness is contained in
nine letters.

Because we borrow a name.

Because we steal a name.

Maybe, we reclaim a name.

Because there is so much in a name.

In this name,
Mardi Gras

In the process of naming,
Mardi Gras

In meaning making,
Mardi Gras

We are making new meanings, and I feel born with excitement as history comes full throttle crash into the present, and we are inside it all, watching an explosion of futures.

Are you coming to Mardi Gras?

I sit back in my chair and my spine clicks with relief. I remember, I used to love this. Back in the library, thinking one day one day one day I'm going to get a scholarship and study literature and be a real writer. It dawns on me that I still love this. That, perhaps, writing was never my way out, but always my way in.

I feel a gushing sense of pride, grab my notebook and run into Marg's room, where Daphne is doing Marg's makeup. Can I read you something? She opens one eye. Sure, she says. I read them what I've written. When I finish, there are tears in Marg's eyes and Daphne says, don't blink, you'll ruin my work! She quickly grabs a tissue and lightly dabs Marg's eyes. Do you like it? I ask. She shakes her head. I love it. Then Daphne says, and in answer to your question, fuck yes, we're coming! Now sit your little arse down, you're next. I shake my head. No way! Oh, come on, says Marg, we're all dressing up! I roll my eyes. *Fine*, but no pink, okay? Daphne grins, and pats the bed next to Marg. I sit down and close my eyes. Marg puts on a record and cracks open beers. I sip my drink between dusts of glitter and eye shadow. When Daphne is done, I have dewy lips and hot pink eyelids that shine like dawn clouds. Don't you go washing it off now, Daphne says as I eye myself in the mirror. I wouldn't dare. Daphne snaps her palette shut. Good. Now what are you wearing?

Daphne dresses me in red leather pants and a red leather corset. My hair is a teased mess. I've got on a pair of Greta's red platform boots. Bloody hell! Dave exclaims when I come down the stairs. I flick him the finger and he and Tony, who are sitting on the couch drinking beers, crack up laughing. Johnny tells me I look hot, and I say, I'm on fucking fire. And I am. My joy is licked flames. As we strut hand in hand towards Taylor Square, I am smiling so wide my cheeks burn.

Out of the bars and onto the streets!

83

Despite the break of winter cold, the crowd on Oxford Street is ablaze. Bodies do that, when they collide. They generate heat. Glittered torsos rub up against feathered necks and the whole street is a hot ache, fanning out.

We chant.

> *Out of the bars and onto the streets!*
> *Out of the bars and onto the streets!*

We scream.

> *Out of the bars and onto the streets!*
> *Out of the bars and onto the streets!*

More and more people are joining us, spilling out of the bars and onto Oxford Street. We swell in numbers, spirit, joy, euphoria. We party towards Hyde Park, in bursts of vibrant colour, hairspray, glitter and pulsating song. Singing and laughing and swaying and kissing. Becoming emboldened, growing louder, riotous as hot hell. So much so that I begin to feel desperately alive, like my body is the underside of a warm, sparkling sea. I am so full of tropical ocean. All coral forest and wild fish. And then I see her and I feel my skin become the thinnest membrane, as if waves of sea foam might breach my flesh and roll out through my chest.

She is dancing, spinning, gliding.

I begin to push through the crowd, past Geoff with Johnny riding on his shoulders, past the back of the truck where Marg and Big Dave and Greta are dancing on the tray, past Daphne swaying with Sam in her diamante-studded dress, to Caragh.

I am just a few shoulders away from her, reaching out for her arm . . .

Then, suddenly, chaos is all at once.

Because we are now being herded from Hyde Park up William Street to the Cross, where cops are waiting along dimmed edges. They are taking off their badges in the shadows . . . Emerging in bright bursts of blue, to slaughter us.

Years from now, I'll remember the sounds of bones breaking. Because they hit us with batons, and we fight back with fists and feet and metal bin lids. And I don't know where to look, where to run, who to fight, because all around me, my friends are being dragged and beaten. So I look up, beyond the buildings, to the sky, and wonder, who is looking back? Who is seeing this? In all our humiliation and heartbreak, who is witnessing *us*?

Get off me! she screams. I look over and see Caragh on the ground, an officer with his fist clenched in her brilliant red hair. And before I can think, my red boot is kicked behind his knee, sending him to the ground, face first against the concrete. Come on! I yell, hoisting her to her feet in a mad scramble. And then we are running. But where? They're everywhere, at the neck of every alleyway. Here, she says, taking my hand. Under here! She pulls me down to the ground and wiggles her way beneath a car. I glance back over my shoulder. Come on! she yells. I nod and follow her under.

From beneath the car, we hear the thuds of wood and metal against flesh. We hear the screams of skin ripped open. The certain cries that spit only from the throats of brutalised bodies. We are close enough to taste the grief on each other's breath. Then Johnny falls to the road beside the car. We lock eyes, and in the moment before two officers grab him by the neck and rip him away, there's a flash of yellow fear. Caragh reaches for his hand, but I stop her. Terrified. I fasten my grip. For her, or for me. I don't know.

She's crying. I half smile and realise I am crying too. Because Johnny's blood sparkles on the road. It's seeping into the bitumen. Hot and viscous. I can smell it, the rusty salt. Like a long iron jetty, stretching into an impossible sea. My tears taste of snot and gasoline. Someone shatters a window and glass rains down like confetti, glittering all around us. She begins to sob. *Shh,* I whisper. Or does she whisper, and I am sobbing?

Our lips touch, hard at first. Then we breathe and soften. Sinking. Into the underland. All grime and gasoline and mucus and blood. Fresh tears like deep ocean, because I am opening. And I believe that I might love her, or that I will love her, because this touch is being held, wholly and entirely. Amongst the gore and the grossness, she kisses me like I am God. Like I am sacred. As if, in this damp darkness, I am the window that's letting the light in, the breath of fresh air she's been blue waiting for. Or at least, she is that for me.

limb two

I AM LYING on the grass in the shadow of the library. Tuesday morning, midwinter. The air is sharp, but the sun is soft on the skin. Thomas walks over with a thermos of hot tea, two cups, and the paper folded under his arm. He sits down beside me and kisses my forehead. I prop myself up on one elbow as he pours out the tea and passes me my cup. I raise it to my lips. Careful, it's hot. He unfolds the paper, blows gently on his tea. Did you hear about this? he asks, turning the paper so I can see the article.

I see a name I recognise printed in a long list of names, occupations and addresses, and think, oh, Jen. I remember her.

Thomas points to another name on the list. *Geoff Bloom.* Didn't he used to work here? he asks.

I think so, I say, I'm pretty sure he taught fine art.

Thomas shakes his head. I can't believe the university would be so reckless as to give someone like *that* a job here, he says. Like, he'd have been teaching young men . . . It's so inappropriate, don't you think?

I take a sip of my tea, but it's still far too hot. The drink scalds my throat and now I'm wincing from the burn in my chest.

You alright? he asks me.

I nod, yeah, I'm okay, just burnt my tongue.

Thomas is in my room for the first time. He's sitting at my desk, thumbing the spines of books I've bought with my scholarship stipend. We're not allowed boys in our room at college, and the thought that we might get caught makes the walls feel swollen, like the space between is becoming tighter, heavier. He exhales and I hear the quiver of his breath and feel a rush of excitement at his nervousness. Thomas picks up the collection of Dylan Thomas poems that he lent me last week. Did you like these?

I nod wordlessly.

My mother named me Thomas because of these, he says. He looks out the window and, after a long pause, says, I sometimes wonder if I only wanted to be a writer because of my name. Or if I would have been one anyway . . . He looks at me now and says, if I was named after a football player, might I have wanted that instead?

I shrug. You don't strike me as much of a football player.

He laughs. No, I guess not.

I touch the bed beside me, smoothing the sheets with my palm, inviting him.

Do you want me to sit next to you? he asks, already blushing.

I nod and he grins, crossing the small space to climb onto my single bed. He sits down, cross-legged, his knee pressed against my shin.

I just think, he says, there is so much in a name.

I touch his open palm with my fingertip. I mean, I say teasingly, a name is just a sound people make with their mouths that we learn to respond to.

He closes his hand around my fingertip and says, but it's more than that ... because that sound signifies *us*. It becomes our identity.

I shake my head. I don't think my identity is in my name.

Thomas frowns. How can it not be? It is the word you start out from. Every word that comes after is shaped by your name. Strung into sentences and formed into paragraphs. At the centre, your name remains the cause of your story. He smiles sheepishly. You're blushing, he says.

I touch my face and feel the warmth of wanting simmering beneath the surface. I tell him, well, you certainly sound like a writer to me.

Thomas edges closer. He touches my jaw with his thumb, and I feel the shake in his hand. Our lips come together in a slow sway. I lightly bite his lip and feel his entire body quake. He touches my throat and I feel a pang of want between my thighs.

I think of a Dylan Thomas poem, of rage and dying light, and feel the word *rage* unshackle from hate, feel it align instead with the ache of desire. Because words are sometimes slippery. Because rage here might mean something else. In the dying light, he takes off my blouse and I feel breathlessly torn apart. And as he undoes his buttons and pulls down his pants, I feel I want all of him around and in me. I want to be engulfed and consumed, swallowed whole.

The word *coming* reads like *arriving*. And I experience this, coming. Because it is the most Holy undoing, with his face wedged between my thighs, tongue flicked wet, my whole body shaken into pieces. I learn that coming starts within and spreads outwards, through the limbs into the fingertips and toes, so that muscles clench tight around bones, so tight I think, I am *breaking*. I arrive, in the moment I am broken. Skin shiny. He kisses me and tells me he loves the way I taste, and I fall back into sheets that stink of sweat and heaved breath.

Coming *is* arriving, I think, and I have, exquisitely, arrived.

I love you, Thomas says.

And I reply, without breath, I love you too. And I do, I love him, I love him, I love him. Because kids get it wrong, and I was just a kid before. I've grown up now. *This* is grown-up love.

limb one

You PUBLISH THE names, occupations and addresses of everyone who got arrested. All fifty-three of them, outed overnight. In the *Sydney Morning Herald*. You, whoever you are, publish their names and occupations and addresses and my friends lose their lives. Not dead, but you bring them to the brink. Because jobs are lost. Marriages are lost. Houses are lost. Kids are lost. You bring them to the brink of drowned, because a person can tread water for only so long.

Uranian House opens its door and those who are drowning wash in, drenched and shaken. We give them towels and chicken soup and wait, anxiously, for the blue to fade from their flesh. And now it's Dave, Tony and Brad camped out in the living room. It's Stella on Marg's couch. It's Greta and her girlfriend Maeve on the floor in my room, Peggy on the floor in Daphne's room. It's Lisa on the couch in Johnny and Geoff's room, Paul sharing a bed with Sam. It's Robin asleep in the bathtub. Uranian House, as it has always been, is the warm calm in the eye of the storm. The reprieve. Here, folks have space to survive. And we do, we survive – against you. We survive, because what else is there?

Caragh is in my room for the first time. She's sitting at my desk, thumbing the spines of the books I've collected from second-hand shops and charity stores. She picks up my notebook and looks at me. My skin is fizzy water, but I say, sure, open it. She reads the first page. This was my sign, she says. I tell her, I know. Caragh asks, is that why you were in the auditorium? And I shrug, silent. This is the first time I've seen her since we huddled together in the gutter outside Darlo police station, singing to our friends inside. And I wonder, if I start to speak, what will I say? That I've long dreamt of her? That I've imagined what she tastes like? That in the darkest corner of my mind, I've already fucked her? Caragh turns the page. Pauses, takes a breath. Then she holds it up so I can see it. *Who is Marcel Moore?* I can tell you, she says, if you want?

I am sitting on my bed, back against the wall. I touch my hand to the sheet beside me, smoothing out the crinkles. Pat the mattress. Caragh leaves the notebook on my desk, steps across Maeve and Greta's mattress on the floor and climbs onto the bed. She sits down, cross-legged, her knee pressed against my shin. I lean my head back against the wall and close my eyes.

She tells me, Marcel's given name was Suzanne. She met Lucette when she was seventeen and Lucette was fourteen. Lucette's mum had been institutionalised for mental illness, and not long after their meeting, Lucette tried to kill herself. Her father was worried she was ill with the same disease that had taken her mother, so he took her to a psychotherapist . . . Caragh is silent for a moment. I hear the quiver in her breath and feel a rush of excitement at her nervousness. Then she says, the psychotherapist said, Lucette is in love with Suzanne, and if you don't let them be together, I fear that she may die . . .

I open my eyes and look at Caragh. Light is slanted gold across her cheek. The doors to my balcony are open. I feel the whole world rushing into this moment. Well, I say, what did he do? Caragh grins. He began chaperoning Lucette to Suzanne's house, where he met Suzanne's mother, a widower. And not long after that, Suzanne's mother and Lucette's father got married. Whether they were in love or not, I don't know. But it meant Suzanne and Lucette became stepsisters. So, they could be affectionate in public, and people assumed it was just sisterly affection . . .

I laugh, out loud, unruly joy bursting from my throat. Caragh nods, touches the inside of my palm with her fingertip. She tells me, they were able to live together, which they did, for more than four decades . . . I clench my hand around Caragh's fingertip. They moved to Paris, she says, where they became Claude and Marcel. Though many academics have omitted their work from anthologies and archives, they were profoundly influential in the formation of the Surrealist movement in France.

I ask her, what did they make? Caragh tells me that Claude wrote, and that Marcel would illustrate the pages. That they photographed and were photographed. That the borders between muse and maker dissolved through their making together. And I get it, because as I lean in to kiss her, I feel, in this moment, as though I am both making and being made.

Later, Caragh will tell me how when Claude and Marcel were living in Nazi-occupied Jersey, they created art with the intention of inspiring dissent among the soldiers. How they punctured and subverted Nazi propaganda pamphlets through collages and word games, and I will feel ripe with potential for what *we* could create.

Later, Caragh will tell me how when Claude and Marcel were caught, they swallowed pills so that they would die together. How they each survived, neither knowing the other had too. How when they were sentenced to death *and* six years hard labour, Claude had joked, will we do the hard labour before, or after, we are executed?

Later, Caragh will tell me how Claude and Marcel made friends with the guards, who eventually let them share a cell. How just before they were to be executed, the war ended, and they walked free. How they continued to make art, even as Claude's health was deteriorating.

Later, Caragh will tell me how when Claude died, Marcel chose the words

AND I SAW NEW HEAVENS AND A NEW EARTH

to be inscribed on her headstone. And I will think to myself, selfishly perhaps, I hope I die first,

because, when we are outside, I learn the sick pleasure of almost kisses, of side glances and wanting smiles. I learn how pining starts

95

between the thighs and spreads outwards, stomach clenched and fingers feeling like shallow light because all the blood is rushing out of them. And it's not that I haven't yearned before. This feeling has been long deep in me, but that now it is swollen with promise and fully realised. Because this yearning is contained in the hour at the markets, or in the waiting for the barman to pour us our beers, and we feel it vibrate between us with such intensity that I want to say, fuck the beers, run with me, home. Because this yearning is felt tenfold knowing that we will soon shut the door behind us. It makes me ache for her with utter desperation. It makes it difficult to concentrate. All the books speak of butterflies, but I feel birds in my stomach, thick-winged and thrashing. I watch her finger her purse for coins at the checkout and imagine her hand fucking me. She notices the thought on my face and bites her lip. Then, when the woman serving us isn't looking, she winks and I feel I might explode through my skin. This is our game, of subtle gestures, a language of limbs written like words in sand. We toe the shoreline between rock and ocean, between what you see and what we are underneath,

because, when we are inside, surrounded by stacked books, dried flowers and dripped wax, we undress. Not just the fabric, but the skin too. Because she tells me that fucking me is like painting the underside of my flesh. A painting that only we bear witness to.

Until one day, in bed and soft light, she will call me Claude. I will smile and call her Marcel. And we will say these names, in private, over and over.

As I fuck her and write her onto the page. As she fucks me and draws me in the margins.

limb two

I GRADUATE WITH a high distinction average and Thomas says, I told you, you're the smartest person I know. The university offers me a scholarship to do honours in English literature, and I think, I really deserve this. I'm a girl from a steel town, the first of my family to go to university. I think of my grandpa, in the mines, dying young, and consider how lucky I am to have escaped the underground. To bask in daylight on sprawling grounds. To lie beneath Moreton Bay figs with a book in hand, imagination brimming. I don't think I'm a writer, despite Thomas's relish for my essays. What I'm good at is picking at and teasing apart sentences, extrapolating, like a miner sieving earth for gold. I'm good at meaning making.

What are you going to research? my mother asks me.

We are sitting in the pub having dinner to celebrate. Mum has splashed out and ordered a bottle of champagne. Thomas and his parents are here too. They speak with accents that sway up and down, like they're singing. After a few beers, his dad, Morgan, has become impossible to understand. They're from a small mining town on the northwest coast of Wales, and bond with my parents over their shared lineage of men working in the dark beneath rock and dirt.

I tell Mum I'm going to research Modernist women writers who, at the turn of the twentieth century, were trying to come up with a woman's way of writing.

Mum frowns. A woman's way . . . what does that mean?

Well, I explain, in the English language at least, men wrote the dictionaries, so they effectively defined and ordered words. And they wrote the stories by which we model *how* to tell a story. I'm going to research how these women made sentences their own . . . Because I think there are specific experiences that men will never be able to write about with the same depth of feeling.

My dad asks bluntly, so you don't think men should write women characters?

Not necessarily, I say, and Dad shakes his head.

I think the mark of a great author is someone who can put themself inside any character, he says.

And I respond, it is difficult for a woman to define her feelings in a language chiefly made by men to express theirs.

Thomas, who is holding my hand under the table, asks, Thomas Hardy?

I grin, say, yep.

Well, it all sounds very smart, Mum says, laughing as she pours the champagne. She turns to Thomas's mother, Gwen. How'd we get so lucky?

I go home to Newcastle for the summer holidays and write, every day, to Thomas. I find the sweetest joy in pining for him, in waiting for him. It makes the days stretch out sideways, growing full with promise, and promises. Thomas, too, writes to me every day, but there is a lag, a gap of time between the letter being posted and the letter getting delivered, and it's in this in-between that I become sure we are made for each other. Because often I find myself answering a question or responding to a train of thought that hasn't arrived yet. And then the letter is in the mailbox that afternoon, affirming I was right to think it. Like when I write to him on Thursday, and pen the words, I can't wait until we live together, and then his letter arrives, dated the previous Monday, with the words, I think we should live together. What do you think?

She no longer lives over the fence. Now she lives overseas, over oceans and mountains, beneath different constellations. Her parents are here, still, and they come over on Boxing Day for prawns on the barbecue and swimming in the pool. They lie on the deckchairs, sipping my dad's famous Bloody Marys, talking about her. I try not to listen, try desperately not to imagine her walking the streets of London, rain as fine as hair catching on the woollen threads of her jumper. I try not to imagine who she might be with, who might be holding her through the long and dark winter, mulled wine and Yorkshire puddings. Who she might lie with on the grass in the long and light summer, daffodils and sweet cider. But the thoughts creep in like a haunting.

I see her, when Mum and I walk through town. She's on the stairs of the town hall with friends. She's coming out of the water on Merewether Beach. She's sitting at the window of the pub. She's not, of course, but I see her anyway. All the ghosts of her make the air of the present thick and hard to swallow. A yearning I had forgotten is, once more, bitter in my throat.

Dear Thomas,

Tell me about your Christmas? What did you eat? Did your parents get drunk? Mine did!

What have you been reading? Are you writing?

For Christmas, Mum gave me Dylan Thomas's Under Milk Wood. *I've started it, but I think you're right . . . it would be best read aloud. Will you read it to me?*

I had a dream last night that we were in Snowdonia. It must have been spring, because there wasn't any snow and there were wildflowers everywhere. We were walking on a mountain path surrounded by lakes and broken rock. For some reason we weren't wearing any shoes, but the ground didn't hurt – not very realistic, I know! But it was wildly beautiful, just like you described to me! I remember the dream so vividly, the feeling of the wind beating against my skin, the yellowed scent of the wildflowers . . . I hope you'll take me there one day! I remember you had Welsh cakes in your pocket, wrapped in a napkin. We sat down on top of the mountain to eat them, but I woke up before I got to taste one. The next time your mum makes Welsh cakes, will you save me one, please?

I cannot wait for the summer to end. I just miss you so much!

All my love, always.

limb one

CARAGH LIVES IN an artists' commune down by the water. The walls are cracked plaster and flaked paint, the ceilings spotted with blooms of damp that swell in the summer. Her room is filled with her art. She paints on wooden boards she's salvaged from scrap yards, sealing them with varnish first so they won't warp from the wetness. Caragh paints the body, over and over, abstracted so that limbs flail and bend in awkward directions, so that you don't know where the body begins and where it ends. Soon, I notice myself emerging in her work and feel thrilled at being seen, at being the subject of her desire. She jokes that it's not me, that I've got such a big head. But when our laughter quietens, she kisses me on the mouth and whispers, it is you. It will always be you.

I tell her, I think I love you. I say *I think* because I am terrified. But she sees straight through me. You *think*? I nod, holding my breath through her long silence until, finally, she says, I love you . . . I love you absolutely and entirely. I exhale an outpour of relief, my whole body shaking, because so often I have felt that futurity does not belong to me, that I am bound to the present, unable to imagine a beyond in which I want to live, but here she is, Caragh, becoming my open future. And I feel undone by the chance of it all, by the years made possible by our being together, by my desire to live into tomorrow, next year, the decade beyond. I kiss her and taste the salt of our tears, and imagine that we are underwater, just us, in the dark and salty depths, learning, again, how to breathe.

We are down on the grass overlooking Sydney Harbour. The water is frilled lichen. We sit apart beneath the gaze of passing straights walking their dogs and exercising in the park. Two women in jeans and thick jumpers stroll past. Caragh makes eye contact with one of them and gently touches my hand. The woman smiles and touches the hand of the woman she's walking with. I feel giddy at the sight of us, of being seen and acknowledged in public. Looking around the park, I say, maybe they're all fucking gay. I mean, who knows? Caragh shakes her head. If everyone is, she says, then no one is. I sit with that thought and look up. Above us, a flock of birds swells and contracts, taking shape and then dispersing. There must be a word for that, she says, pointing to the sky. There is, I say, it's a murmuration. Caragh says it slowly back to me, *murmuration*, letting the word roll gently off her tongue. That might just be my favourite word, she says as she looks at me and smiles, her skin flashing like wet gold.

Caragh is naked in my bed, drawing with pastels. I am at my desk writing. I look across and see her deep in her work, tongue bit with concentration. I drink in the hazy pink light, the curve of her hip, the rush of her hand across the paper, turn back to the page and the words fall out of me.

our history has been burnt and burnt again / yet, here we are / again
here / we / are / indulging

and I want you to / indulge / I want you / to suck / to chew / to slurp / to devour / banquet on me / feast on me / eat me / *alive!*

tell me now / the price of salt?

you say, we are the love that dare not speak its name.

I say, here we are, burning.

we are burning in love.

I look up from the page, to her. She is holding up her drawing; a blue murmuration moves over a blood-orange sky. She asks, can you read me what you've written?

We fuck, slow and soft, hard and with haste, exploring the borders of our bodies. Sometimes, I close my eyes and see her in the desert at the edge of the sun, see her in the bush running between spotted gums, see her diving down the side of a coral atoll, see her falling through a blue-green glacier. Other times, I keep my eyes open and see her body shimmer with sweat like a fish belly, see her lips, stained pink with my blood as she exposes my abjection.

Always, I am listening to her and chasing the sound. Finding her, at last, in a rush of hot breath, coming back to the room of the present. Lying together, unsure where one body ends and the other begins, I tell her, we create and bear witness, that is what we do for each other. Caragh smiles and kisses my throat. And then we start, all over again.

We are sitting on my balcony in our underwear. She is wearing one of my shirts, unbuttoned. I have a denim jacket hooked over my shoulders. Caragh lights her cigarette. She passes me the matches and I light mine. She draws, exhales, tells me the police are kicking everyone out. The government wants to knock down their house for a train line, or an overpass, she isn't quite sure. You can move in here if you want, I tell her. Do you want that? she asks me. You're here all the time anyway, I say. I know, she says, but do you want me to live with you? I nod, yes . . . don't you? Yes, she says, I want to live here. It's just, the way you said it, you sounded unsure. I shrug and tell her, I've never lived with a partner before. Me either, she says. To be honest, I say, I'm scared I'll fuck this up. Terrified, actually. She says, well that makes two of us.

limb two

WE LIVE NOW in a tiny studio apartment at the back of Darlinghurst. Our parents don't know we've moved in together. While we're still studying, this is all we can afford. Sometimes the hot water doesn't run, but we decorate the walls with our drawings and handwritten poems, so that we are wrapped in the paper warmth of our cocoon. Filled each morning with light streaming in through the wide window over the kitchen sink, and a skylight above us, we bathe in sunshine, naked and entwined. The studio is smaller than my room at college, but it's a weight off, to be in here, with him, in the undisturbed quiet. Lounging and reading in amber light. Brewing tea and making scrambled eggs with butter. The place smells like lavender soap and worn books and ink. Our bed is a mattress on the floor, and sometimes we stay there all day. Heads in the pages, bodies caressing, as birdsong gives way to blue shadow and I slip, gently, then all at once —

she opens the door – slushy brown snow – sleek ice – you must be freezing – quick – come inside – I follow her down a hallway down a staircase – into the basement – we are beneath the street now – in the quiet glow – art on the walls but I can't make out the pictures – candles flicker on the bookshelf – coat **is damp** – here – take this off – she slips her hands beneath the **shoulders** of my coat and slides it off – it's warm down here – I am trembling – skin pricked because here she is after all this time saying I thought you'd never come – I tell her I'm here I'm right here! – she touches my hip bone – my singlet – I raise my arms so she can lift it over my head – nipples hard as she kisses them as I take her shirt off as I kiss her as we collapse onto the floor as she pulls down my pants as she touches me as the candle tips over as the bookshelf catches fire as the words burn and cover our skin in ash –

as I wake –

in a burst of breathy panic and Thomas turns on the lamp to look at me, startled and concerned. You're crying, he says, are you okay?

I nod, barely able to breathe, sobbing quietly as he wraps me in his body and whispers, *shh*, it was just a nightmare, you're safe now.

As my cries soften I whisper, I want to marry you.

When he touches me, I feel like I am being turned inside out, like he's writing on the underside of my flesh. A private story that only we read. Did you mean it? he asks me, as he enters my body. When you said you want to marry me, did you mean it?

I cradle his cheek with my open palm as he moves deeper into me. I did, I say, I do. I mean it. I want to marry you.

His torso is pressed hard against mine as he moves in and out, bringing us both to the brink until we're over the edge and falling. Collapsing into the sheets, he kisses my neck for a long moment. Then he reaches, out of the bed, and across the floor to his jeans pocket where he pulls out a box. Opening it, he kneels before my spread legs, both of us shaking as he whispers, will you marry me?

I start to cry. I say, yes, yes of course, yes! And then he starts crying, too, and I think, this is perfect, so perfect. This is how it's supposed to be.

limb one

CARAGH AND I come home to find Greta on the floor in our bedroom, barely able to breathe. Her face is bright red as she looks up, her cheek already shiny. Oh my God, Caragh says, fuck. She kneels down, wipes Greta's matted hair off her face, takes it gently between two palms, kisses her forehead. *Shh*, she whispers, you're safe . . . Slowly Greta's cries soften. Deep breaths, says Caragh. Ready, in, out. I watch them inhaling and exhaling together and feel my skin become pricked by shivers. I can't take my eyes off the bruise on Greta's cheek. I get a whiff of freshly cut grass and feel like I might vomit. I need a smoke, I say, and leave the room before Caragh has a chance to say anything.

My hands are shaking in the kitchen as I try to roll a cigarette. In the yard, between overgrown ivy, passionfruit and twinkling fairy lights, I strike a match, light and inhale, but the smoke does little to calm me because the stream of memory is swift and relentless. I shuffle over to the bushes at the corner of the yard and throw up until I'm dry. There are footsteps behind me. I wipe my mouth and turn around. What's going on? asks Caragh.

I want to tell her, tell her everything, but the truth is impossibly heavy. It sits in me like a dead thing. Like a dead bird, feathers matted, in the pit of my belly. I feel disgusting when I think of it, and so I don't. I swallow and say, nothing, nothing is going on.

Come here, she says, and helps me to a chair at the outdoor table. I'll get you some water . . . She leaves and returns with a glass. I sip the water, sloshing it around in my mouth, then spit it on the pavers beside us. That got on my shoe, she says, grinning. I ask Caragh, when did you come out? She shrugs, all the time? No, I say, like the first time . . . like, to your parents? Caragh laughs, but the sound is edged by grief. My parents, she says, are Irish Catholics. I will never come out to them. I feel myself frowning. They don't know about you? She shakes her head. But you see them all the time, I say. What about your brothers? She shakes her head again. They don't know either, she says.

I think sometimes of the 'closet', the place, the word and its attachments. A closet, after all, is a small space. It exists within a home, but it is starved. There is no light in there, no air, no room to fuck, no place to sleep. It is safe, for a time, perhaps. But a body in there will erode. Until its flesh is all gone and it becomes a secret of bones. To come out is to escape the secret, to stretch your limbs and bathe your skin in light. Sometimes. Because to come out can also be a sharper death, a quicker death. Total obliteration.

Either way, to come out is always the end of something.

I ask Caragh, don't you feel bad? She responds sharply, no. I say, but you're hiding who you are. You're lying to them . . . Caragh frowns now. My mother, she says, genuinely believes gay people burn in hell. And I love her . . . Before I think it through, I rebut, but how can you love someone who wouldn't accept you . . . the *whole* of you? Caragh's eyes become glassy. She wipes them on her sleeve. I don't want my mum to die one day thinking that she won't find me again in heaven. I shrug and look down into my lap, playing with my ring. She says, you don't understand, do you? I shake my head. It's a lie, Caragh, I tell her. She bites her lip. Finally, she says, no, it's not . . . it's a gift. When I don't respond, Caragh asks, what about you, then? I feel my jaw clench. Her tone has shifted. When did you come 'out', as you say?

I think of my before, a whole other life, a dead thing. I've never told this story, not to anyone, not even Dave. I feel my limbs stiffen, choked cold. Caragh's demeanour shifts again, softening this time. She takes hold of my hand. I see it, her hand, touching mine, but I can't feel it. I can't feel anything. There's the scent again, of freshly cut grass. Terror courses through my body. It makes everything feel weightless and floaty, like I'm up between the ivy and the flickering lights, watching myself, down there, holding hands with the love of my life. I observe my body, rigid as marble. You're so strong. You're so strong! Look at how strong you are! What I never imagined is how much I would have liked to have remained soft.

I can't, I finally hear myself say. She sighs and says, okay, and I see a fissure crack open in the space between us. I want to shake myself silly, scream into my face, what are you so afraid of? Why won't you tell her? *Tell her!* But she has already gone inside.

Greta sleeps in our bed between Caragh and me. A few times, in the night, she wakes and cries against our bodies. Caragh holds her, stroking her hair. I turn so my back is against them, eyes open.

When dawn breaks, Caragh makes a pot of coffee. We drink it in bed, the three of us, smoking cigarettes. Greta looks at her watch, says, better get to work. Caragh frowns and asks, are you sure you're okay to go? Greta nods, it'll be a good distraction. Then she stubs out her cigarette in the shell we're using for an ashtray and climbs out of bed. I watch her apply powder to the blue of her bruise, dusting over the hurt.

There's the feeling of hot bitumen, of sore feet bleeding, of wandering, of wondering, when will this end? The scent of freshly cut grass. Caragh touches my hand, and I look up, at the walls we've adorned with poetry and drawings, at the soft swathes of sunlight. Where did you just go? she asks me. I exhale smoke, pull my hand away from her. Nowhere, I say.

Caragh puts a match to the end of her cigarette. Poor thing, she says, I hope she's okay. I ask, did Greta tell you what happened? Caragh nods, nursing her mug of coffee. Greta kissed someone. Who? I ask. Caragh takes a sip, then a drag of her cigarette. A man she works with . . . I think the baker. They kissed out the back of the bakery, and Greta told Maeve last night. I say, holy shit. Caragh nods, yeah, well they got into a huge fight and Maeve hit her. I look down at my coffee, swirling the mug in my hand. So, I say, Greta is bisexual? Caragh frowns. You sound surprised. I am, I tell her. I mean, did Maeve know that? Caragh says bluntly, I don't know. She takes a long drag of her cigarette, blowing it out with force.

There is a moment, now, somewhere here, that I will agonise over in days to come. Somewhere between me saying, no wonder Maeve was angry, and Caragh getting out of bed.

Maeve *hit* her, says Caragh, glaring at me with eyes so sharp they could slice me open.

I lean my head back against the wall and observe her, by the window, half naked, fingers trembling. She smokes in silence until, finally, she stubs out her cigarette and slips it into an empty wine bottle, turns to me and asks, what if I was? I meet her gaze. What if you were what? Bisexual, says Caragh. I laugh. She shudders, shakes her head. You gonna hit me now? Don't be ridiculous, I say. I know you're not . . .

Caragh says, fuck you.

And then she's at the bookshelf, pulling books off. She's at our desk, gathering her pastels and her papers. She's in our closet, ripping dresses and shirts off their hangers. And I am here in our bed, breathlessly here, watching myself watching Caragh as she pulls our life apart. Silent. Desperately silent. Until she's no longer here, until she's gone and I'm staring at our half-empty room, at all the missing pieces, wandering between the balcony and the desk, wondering, hopelessly, how do I go back?

I write her letters and then burn them. Maybe that's it, eh?

limb two

OUR APARTMENT GETS broken into one morning when we are both at university. There are few things to steal, but it's obvious someone has been here because our closet is emptied, clothes strewn across the floor. They've taken our kettle and our toaster, and the fifty dollars we'd saved in my underwear drawer. I feel sick at the thought of someone rifling through my undies. I start to sob.

Thomas says, hey, *shh*, it's okay . . .

He rubs between my shoulder blades.

I'm being ridiculous, I say, I'm sorry.

You've got nothing to be sorry for. I'm just glad you weren't here.

I ask, can we sleep with the light on tonight?

Sure, he says and kisses me on the cheek.

We go to the police station and to our relief, two officers arrive at our apartment the very next morning, one writing in his notebook while the other advises us to replace our locks. Thomas says, I'd offer you a tea, but they stole our kettle.

The officer smiles sweetly and says, unfortunately there's been a few break-ins recently. You did the right thing by reporting this.

The second officer notices me playing with the ring on my finger. Recently engaged? he asks.

Yeah, I say, blushing.

Congratulations, he says.

Yes, adds the first officer, congrats.

After they leave, Thomas says, they were nice, weren't they?

Yes, I tell him, they were very kind.

You feeling alright? he asks as he takes me in his arms.

I surrender to his body, softening in his embrace. Yeah, I say, I'm feeling much better now.

limb one

I ASK FOR her, everywhere. I ask everyone, have you seen Caragh? How's she doing? They tell me, she's pretty mad. They tell me, she doesn't want to talk to you. Johnny says, I'll tell you a little secret . . . Caragh doesn't feel like she knows you. To which I laugh, and he shakes his head and takes hold of my hand. I'm serious, Little Dave. He pinches my skin. Your walls are made of ice. They always have been, ever since Big Dave brought you in here as that angry little kid. I pull my hand away, tell him he's wrong. Tell him, Johnny, you don't know anything! Johnny shrugs, yeah, maybe that's the problem . . .

Marg tells me Johnny's right. I roll my eyes. Oh, come on, I say, don't you start too. Hey, Marg says as she puts down a glass and slings the tea towel she's holding over her shoulder. Show some respect, she says. Daphne weighs in and tells me, believe it or not, we're a lot older than you. We've been around these parts since before you were potty trained. So, you best be remembering who you're talking to. I resign, fine. I'm all ears! Marg sighs.

She leans across the bar and takes my hand. You know, people out there, a lot of them really do want us dead. They want to see us in pain. And you know what fucks them off the most? I shrug and she shakes my hand. When we *love*! Daphne nods in agreement and says, exactly. So don't be giving in to what the world outside wants for you. Marg remarks, you told me this girl's the love of your life, yeah? I nod. Then start acting like it, ya little shit. Because you don't know what tomorrow will bring. And she's here, right here, today.

It pains me to hear Marg say this, knowing what she's lost. But before I can think to respond, two police officers come into the bar and Marg and Daphne bite their tongues. One cop is tall with spindly limbs, like a spider. His irises are such a pale shade of blue that in the red haze of the bar, they blend with the whites of his eyes, making his pupils appear freakishly pointed. The other cop is bloated and pink faced. Johnny asks, back already? Then, flirtatiously, he grins and says, you just can't get enough of me. Can you? The cop's face gets even redder as he stammers, shut up. *Boy.* Johnny purses his lips, opens the cash register and begins counting the bribe in one-dollar notes. Marg says, in a hushed voice, you wanna get flogged, cuz? *Again?* Johnny ignores her and continues counting out the one-dollar notes. Fine, says Marg, louder and sterner now. Why don't you ask them for a left hook instead of a right this time? Get your nose smashed back into place? Johnny flinches. Yeah, says Marg. Pull ya head in. Johnny finally relents and slips larger notes into an envelope to make up the sum, handing it over. The cop takes it with his meaty hand, shoves the fat envelope into his back pocket. He grunts, then nods to his partner and they head out of the bar as brazenly as they entered.

When they're gone, Marg leans over and clips Johnny around the ear. What the fuck was all that? Johnny holds up a one-dollar note. This is David Malangi's, he says, pointing to the artwork on the note. Only it's been bastardised. Because David didn't know the bank had printed his painting until he saw it already on the one-dollar note. And so, I thought if they wanna steal from us, I'll pay 'em in shit they've already stolen.

limb two

Thomas comes with me to the English Faculty to hand in my honours thesis. Above us, the sky is as blue as the neck of a bluethroat bird. We walk through the dry heat of late November, sun on our shoulders. The university's lawns are sprawling and lush, bordered by beds of imported flowers. My dissertation, now that the pages are collated and bound together, weighs more than I expected. I clutch the work to my chest as Thomas takes a photo of me on his Pentax. The pages feel meaty and full in my hands. I am grinning so wide my face is pinched hurt, but it feels good, so good, like I have truly accomplished something. I think of the hours spent toiling away in the library after dark with my thermos of black coffee, and think, I did it. I really did it. I learnt something. I contributed something to a conversation that exists outside and beyond our tiny apartment. And it doesn't matter to me in this moment who reads it, because as Thomas kisses me on the steps of the English Faculty and tells me, this is your best work yet, I feel so swollen with this achievement. Because I asked a question, and I found an answer. I really proved something, to myself, if no one else.

We meet our parents at a pub opposite Broadway. It's an old worker's pub with sticky carpet and dimmed lights. Mum is annoyed that they don't have champagne, so she buys a bottle of sparkling wine and apologises for it as she pours a glass for me and another for Gwen.

It's fine, Mum, I can't tell the difference anyway.

Oh, I know, she says, laughing as she pours herself a glass. I just wanted it to be special!

I look around the table. At Mum and Gwen all dressed up in their Sunday best, lipstick and pearls. At Dad and Morgan and Thomas, in button-up shirts, hair combed, pants pressed, clinking their beers together.

This is special, I tell Mum. It's perfect.

Well, good, she says. We're all so proud of you!

They raise their glasses to me, and then Thomas, pink-cheeked and gushing, says, it's really very good. Her dissertation. I read every draft.

I correct him by saying, you *helped* with every draft.

Thomas shakes his head. I barely did anything. He turns to my parents, says, it's brilliant.

My dad pipes up. So is that what you'll do now? You'll be a writer?

I shake my head. Oh no, I don't want to write, I want to be a publisher . . . I think I'm good at extrapolating . . . you know?

Dad shakes his head. You lost me with the big words, love.

I'm good at reading a text and mining the gold in it . . .

Ah! he says, laughing. I do know a thing or two about mining.

Morgan laughs with him.

Thomas whispers in my ear, they think they're *so* funny!

I giggle and squeeze his hand under the table.

Now? he whispers.

I nod.

Thomas clears his throat. We actually have something to tell you . . . He points to Gwen and says, I'm surprised *you* didn't notice, Mam, since you're always banging on about it.

Gwen raises her eyebrows. Notice what?

I put my hand out, waving it around the table. The light catches the diamond, throwing small stars across the wall.

Gwen shrieks, oh my *God*! Thomas!

And then my mother bursts into tears. Christ! she splutters, sobbing. This is just the best news! Congratulations! She grabs my face and plasters a sloppy kiss across my cheek.

Well, we need to start planning, says Gwen.

Oh no, says Thomas, we've planned it all already.

We want to keep it simple, no frills.

My dad makes a joke about his wallet liking the sound of this and my mum shoots him a stern look.

We're going to go to Town Hall next week, says Thomas, and we'd like for you all to be there.

Town Hall? Mum says, doing little to hide her dissatisfaction. Why not a church? I've heard of a lovely little church outside–

I cut her off. But we're not religious, Mum. And neither is Thomas.

Yes, I know, but it's tradition . . . I worry you'll get bad luck or something.

I laugh. I'm not worried about that.

Well, will you wear a dress at least?

I sigh. Sure. There's a really great charity store near our building, I was thinking of–

This time Gwen cuts me off. Fy nghariad, she says, shaking her head.

I look to Thomas. He leans across and whispers, it means, my love.

Let your mam and I take you dress shopping, Gwen says.

Please, my mum adds, let us.

I resign. Okay. Sure. But no frills, okay?

The sky is a tired grey above me as I wait for Gwen and Mum outside the flagship David Jones store on Elizabeth Street. They're both late, so I walk past the huge glass windows, staring at mannequins displaying the season's latest fashions. Every window looks as if it's a page in a magazine. Spring outfits complete with beautiful hats, handbags and leather shoes. On one mannequin, a blush pink neckerchief contrasts against an arrangement of green foliage. On another, a houndstooth dress and matching bucket hat clash spectacularly with a floral wall-paper background. Each installation is a work of art, a diorama degustation. Gwen finds me eyeing a blood-orange handbag and says, I've always loved coming to see these windows . . . When we first moved here, I would bring Thomas into the city every holiday to see the Christmas window displays. He just loved them! She grins and tells me, I've always wondered who dresses the windows. She pauses, contemplating, then says, whoever it is, they have the eye, that's for sure.

I agree, smiling. Yeah, they certainly do.

Then she says, I remember there was a department store in Cardiff that I walked past as a young girl with my mam and tad.

It had windows like this. And I remember being enamoured, so completely in awe I was . . . When we went back home to my village, for years I was drawing all kinds of beautiful outfits. I thought I wanted to be a fashion designer . . . She laughs now, as if the very idea was ludicrous.

I ask, why didn't you?

Gwen says, I got married.

Mum cries when I walk out of the change rooms and say, yep, this is the one.

Oh spia del, Gwen says, all rosy-cheeked and glassy-eyed. You look lovely.

I turn and look at myself in the mirror, relieved that after trying on dresses for more than an hour, I've finally found one I feel comfortable in. The dress is soft lace across my collarbones, a simple bust, and a modest skirt that hangs effortlessly, cutting off just below the knee. I look at my body, at the way it is held by the fabric, and imagine how Thomas will feel when he sees me, his wife.

The image is tender, like gentle hands. Tender, like a bruise. It is two things at once, because as I breathe in, I imagine another picture, another story, unfolding somewhere else. Are you okay? Mum asks, eyeing me suspiciously.

I nod and exhale, forcing my breath out of my body, and with it, the thought of her.

limb one

I WALK INTO Daphne's room one morning without knocking. She shrieks, half naked in her underwear, a bra, slippers on and a towel around her head. I told you not to do that! Sorry, I say, flopping down on her bed. I light a cigarette. Daphne, I don't know what to do . . . I fucked it and I don't know what to do. Well, Daphne says sharply, you could start by knocking. I roll my eyes and get off her bed, go to her door, knock three times. Oh! she sings theatrically, my Little D! I've been expecting you, please, come on in! I lie back down on her bed. She asks for a drag of my cigarette, then keeps it, so I roll another. How's your heart? she asks me. Fine, I whip. Daphne, who is sitting in front of her art deco dresser, applying her make-up, looks at me in the mirror, raising one eyebrow in a high, dramatic arc. Do you want my advice or not? Of course I do . . . Well, she says again, how is your heart? I don't know! I snap. Sore? What do you want me to say? She puts her lipstick down and turns to face me. Have I ever told you why I named myself Daphne? I shake my head.

There's a story, says Daphne, in Ovid's *Metamorphoses*, where Apollo is accidentally shot with Cupid's arrow. It makes him lust after Daphne. And not in a beautiful way. This arrow makes him want to consume her, it makes him so besotted that he wants *all* of her, all to himself. She knows his desire will obliterate her, and so, she begins to run. Full of terror, she runs from this being that will eat her alive. She runs for her life. Daphne runs through the forest, Apollo close behind. She runs and runs and runs until she hits a river, and with nowhere to go, she screams for help. And you know what? Someone listens, and they cast a spell to transform her into a laurel tree. And as she sinks her roots, she takes the shape of something else. A different body, yes, but it is a body she can live in, where she can grow and flower and blossom. A body that is hers . . .

Daphne slowly rises from her chair. She stands tall and defiant, strong rooted and flowering. Then she says, I arrived here to survive myself. Do you understand, Little D? I *became* here, to survive myself.

I taste tears on my lips and realise I am crying. Daphne crosses the room to sit beside me. She gently wraps her arm around my shoulder. I bury my face into her neck and sob hard against her skin. There, there, she whispers, quieter than I've ever heard her speak to me before. Honey, she says, there will always be forces that try to obliterate us. But Caragh sees you, and she wants you in the most beautiful way. Don't be afraid of her love, because it's not going to obliterate you. She is here to bear witness. And she knows she can't do that if you don't let her learn who you are.

limb two

– I MOVE SWIFTLY through soft grass – long tufts of it bending in the
breeze like rolling swells of open ocean – running and running –
barefoot – to the edge of a rocky cliff where I see Thomas – a
silhouette – waiting for me – beyond him a blistering sun bleeds
out across water whipped gold and glistening – the wind is in my
hair – I feel released and wild – running and running until I reach
the edge and he turns and I see in the day's dying light – her – it's
her – it's *always* been her – I feel this sunset flood my lungs – feel it
in me softhearted and warm – she takes hold of my hand – smiles –
eyes watery pink – and then she leaps out into the sky – pulls me
with her – glorious – freefalling into a sparkling sea –

I wake in a splash and see Thomas stirring on the pillow beside me.

He opens one eye, grinning. Good morning, he whispers.
And then he says, today . . . you'll become my wife.

I kiss him, because I can't wait.

I get ready with my parents in their hotel room down by the Quay. Mum says, I still can't believe you didn't stay with us last night. You know you're not supposed to stay with your fiancé the night before the wedding.

Says who? I ask as she blushes my cheek with powder.

Oh, I don't know! That's just what they say.

Yeah, well I don't think you're meant to live together either and I haven't been smote yet.

Dad, who is sitting by the window in an armchair drinking a whiskey, laughs at this. He turns to say something and my mum shrieks, don't look! We're not finished her make-up.

Okay, I'll just go back to watching the ferries, then, will I?

Yes, my mum whips.

Great . . . It's riveting stuff, these ferries.

I grin and Mum tells me I'm making this difficult.

Sorry, I mouth, as she applies my lipstick.

Almost ready, Mum says, as she helps me into the dress and does up the back buttons.

Okay, Dad, I say. You can look now.

He turns and I watch his hard exterior crease. Oh . . . he says, eyes watering. Just look at you.

We arrive outside Town Hall and Mum kisses me on the cheek. See you in there, she says, and then she disappears into the building, where the love of my life is waiting with his parents.

Okay then, Dad says. We're doing this. We're really doing this.

Oh, come on, Dad, I say. I'm the one getting married!

He chuckles, then he points up. Look, he says.

I see a flock of birds flying high above, against a creamy sky. They bend and swerve, swelling and contracting.

That's called a murmuration, he says. It's a sign.

A good one?

He hugs me. Yeah, love, he says, a good one.

The room is smooth varnished wood and soft eggshell-blue walls. Thomas is waiting with his parents on one side of the celebrant. My mum is standing on the other. When we enter, Thomas turns to face me. He's wearing a navy blue suit and a pressed white shirt. He looks so handsome, so beautifully open. I watch him witness me, drinking all of me in. I watch him swallow me whole and then smile. There you are.

The celebrant, Sam, is funny in a self-deprecating way that makes us feel instantly at ease. He tells us how he got his bald head sunburnt on purpose, just for us, so that his blue eyes would shine for our wedding. I can already tell my mum is less than impressed by Sam. Later, she'll complain that he reeked of *marijuana* – enunciating the word in such a stuck-up way that Thomas and I have to laugh.

Sam says, Thomas, I now invite you to read your vows.

Thomas pulls a square of paper from his pocket and slowly unfolds it, hands shaking.

Sam says, this better be good, I heard you're a real writer.

Thomas blushes. Let's hope so, he says and clears his throat. Love, I think, is both a coincidence and a choice. You're walking alone along a mountain path, one you're familiar with, one you've gotten to know by now . . . its scent, its texture underfoot . . . and you're used to your own pace, your body's rhythm. So, it comes as a surprise, perhaps, when your path converges with another . . . Because now you're looking at this other traveller, and she starts telling you a story, arranging words in ways that excite you, because you never would have thought to tell a story this way. And so, you decide . . . you make a choice, to walk with her, to hold her hand and tread a new path, one you can forge together. Life, I believe, is a constant wandering. And if you're lucky, you come across someone you want to wander with. I am so full of joy that our paths have crossed, and that I get to walk, now, with you, into our future. I love you, and I promise to be with you, through every grief and every pleasure . . . to walk with you, always, for as long as we shall live.

I look at Thomas through glassy eyes, feeling like the walls of my heart have become soft and honeycombed. All the love I am capable of oozes out into my limbs.

Sam says, well, I'm sorry I made you go second, darling. That'll be a tough act to follow.

We all laugh as Mum passes me my vows. I unfold the paper, take a deep breath and look at Thomas. I never imagined this day. I never imagined getting married, or the dress I'd wear, or the building I'd get married in. I never imagined any of it . . . Not until I met you and felt, for the first time in my life, like I want to live forever. You make me want to live into tomorrow and the next, because each day with you is a quiet joy. I love that we go out for dinner and both sit at the table in silence reading books. I love that you share your words with me, and that I share mine with you, and that together, we make something of each other's lives. Most of all, I love waking up next to you, wondering, what will we come up with today? And so, today, and every day, I promise to be creative with you and with the life we build together . . . to remain curious and inspired. I promise to support you and to not spoil the endings of the books I finish first. Thomas, I love you . . . and I will lean courageously into my future for as long as you're in it.

limb one

'POETRY IS SOMETIMES a no'

My voice feels quiet small in all these imaginings / imagining
now / where you are / where you touch / where you laugh and
take a deep breath / light your cigarette

Maybe / I could say / my heart is quiet small, too / because
someone says, 'paw paw skies' and it feels so soft in the mouth
that I just want to tell you about it / and everything else / because
there is an everything else

There's an everything unfolding somewhere / and I want to see
that / live out all that unfolding / shiny like sweat on bodies /
I want to be there / in that unfolding / in all that unfolding / over
and over again

Someone else says 'poetry is sometimes a no' / in that way,
perhaps we are this poem / perhaps we are our own poetry of

contained almosts / of almost openings / of never quite, but wanting

Someone says 'poetry is deeply humiliating' and I think this is true / in part / humiliating and humility / perhaps these words share a root?

Because prose is unravelling / a story unfolding / and this is constrained and contained / in a moment on a page / bordered by negative space of the unseen and imagined / humiliating, but learning, humility / poetry is silence / it is finite / it is surrender / a value system

Poetry / is sometimes a no

Daphne and Dave agree to give Caragh this poem, and as I watch them walk out through the front door, a great calmness comes over me. Because this poem is silence, it is finite, it is surrendering to Caragh, my muse and maker. When they return, Dave asks how I feel, and I tell him, honestly, I feel calmer now. Daphne laughs, says, I would not feel calm if I gave that poem to someone. But I'm glad you do.

limb two

We borrow Gwen and Morgan's Ford Cortina for our honeymoon. It's pale blue. Like your eyes, I tell Thomas. We pack a tent, sleeping bags, a box of food, and head south. We get lost twice leaving Sydney, pulling into a dead end for the second time and laughing at our hopelessness. Then we see a sign for Wollongong and know we're on the right stretch. We smoke a pack of Camel cigarettes, windows down, radio blaring. Neither of us really smokes at home, but the act of smoking now makes us feel far away from the city, like we could be in any corner of the world. We stop at a roadside stall to buy trays of local peaches and cherries from a sprightly farmer in an Akubra who congratulates us when we say, giggling, that we're on our honeymoon. Then we get back in the Cortina and make sticky messes of ourselves, sweet peach juice trickling down our forearms and chins.

We find a cove on the map called Honeymoon Bay and decide to make it our first stop. How could we not? I say, mouth full of peach. It's literal poetry.

Thomas laughs and says, it'd be rude not to. He flicks the indicator and takes the turn-off, down a road that winds through giant gums. Light falls through the canopy, showering us in splintered gold. I hang my head out the window and breathe in the rush of eucalypt, the dry heat of the bush, beaming at the splendour of it all. When I glance back at Thomas, he looks across at me and smiles. Sometimes, I can't believe you're mine, he says.

And I feel rapture at the thought of being entirely absorbed, of letting go of myself to become part of him. It's a relief, I think, to be held like this.

We pull up at the campsite and wander down a path that opens out onto Honeymoon Bay – a pearl-shaped cove nestled between two arms of pebble and tree, as if the land is holding the water in a warm and gentle embrace. At its outer edge, there is a narrow opening to the wide ocean beyond. The small sea inside the cove is opalescent, a turquoise I've never seen before. Whoa, I exclaim.

This reminds me of Pembrokeshire, Thomas says.

Do you miss it?

He nods. I do, yeah. Very much.

Will you take me one day?

I'd love nothing more.

We pitch our tent and build a fire and sit together in silence, in smoke and fading light, reading. Occasionally, one of us will come across a sentence that we want to share, and we'll pause our quiet ventures to give a line to the other.

I have a question for you, I say over the fire, its embers floating up like small stars.

He looks up from his novel. Yeah?

Do you think poetic language should give away its meaning? Like, should it be easily read and understood? Or should the poet make the work obscure, the meaning more difficult?

Thomas thinks about this for a long time. Well, he says at last, the latter requires education. It requires a knowledge of history and device to decipher the meaning. The former is more accessible, and therefore, I think, more generous. Thomas pauses, then asks me, what do you think?

I agree it is more giving. I think that the reader's context . . . their education, their life experience, their interests, et cetera, will determine the meaning of the work. It's all relative, and therefore the art itself is fluid, it's in a constant state of flux, because the meaning of said art changes depending on who is taking it in and what they bring to the reading.

Thomas considers this, and then he says, I don't want someone to require a degree in literature to be able to understand the meaning of my work . . .

And I feel, in this moment, like I could not love him more.

limb one

It is late afternoon when there's a knock at my bedroom door. Come in, I say. Caragh walks in, poem in hand. Can I sit down? I smile. Yeah, of course.

I tell her the story, the whole way through. I was fifteen and . . . in the garden shed, kissing my neighbour . . . my best friend. She was really beautiful. She had her hand inside me, and I felt like I was being opened, like I'd been looking backwards my entire life, and now someone was showing me my future. Then my mum opened the door and screamed. By the time my dad arrived, she was gone. I never saw her again . . . I never saw any of them ever again, because my dad dragged me out into the yard, by the throat, and punched me in the face.

Caragh touches her hand to my face, caressing my cheek, softly. She leans over and brushes her lips across my wet skin, and as she kisses the groove beneath my eye, I feel something inside me dislodge. It's these words, I realise . . . words that I have held for almost ten years, stored deep in muscle . . . And now they are let go. I feel them, dissolving into my blood like ice into ocean.

I tell her how I ran away, how I roamed the streets for days, until Dave walked up to me beside a petrol station and put me in his truck and gave me a bottle of Coke. Caragh grins, and I tell her how he took me down into the bar and introduced me to Johnny and Daphne, and they brought me here. She smiles. Uranian House . . . Do you know why it's called that? I nod. Daphne says that a sexologist coined the term Uranism to describe patients whose souls did not match their anatomy, and Ruby, who bought this house in the fifties, decided that was who this house was for . . . the Urnings of Uranian House. Caragh takes a drag of my cigarette, then kisses me on the mouth. We taste of salt and damp tobacco. One of Claude Cahun's first publications was titled *Les Jeux Uraniens*, she says. Can you guess what it means? I shake my head and she smiles. It means Uranian Games.

In burnt light she lifts my shirt over my head and kisses my belly, her hands cradling my hip bones; she pulls down my shorts, taking my underwear with them. Tenderly, Caragh brushes her lips from the inside of one thigh to the other, teasing. She grins. And then she takes me in her mouth, pulling me into myself. She gently enters my body to make love to me. Like peeling a fruit slowly with bare hands, Caragh turns me inside out. I close my eyes and imagine her running with me to the edge of a cliff. We catch ourselves at its edge and look out to a wide-open ocean, whipped gold and glistening. She reaches for my hand, and

I let her take me over the edge, freefalling, as we plunge into this sparkling sea. I open my eyes as she collapses onto my torso, all bubbling and warm.

When I regain my breath, I tell her, when we make love, I like that we're the same . . . that I touch you and know how it feels, because you're touching me the same. Caragh sighs. We are the same, she says, but we are also different. Two things can be true at once. I let go and tell her honestly, I've always felt like it was us against the world, and I guess I felt betrayed, or something. Caragh says, you can't put me on a pedestal. If you put me all the way up there, you're not really seeing me. I let these words sink in and realise she's right, I haven't seen her, not really. I look at the way orange light is cradling her breasts. At the folds of her belly. At the thighs I want, always, wrapped thick around my body. Caragh says, I haven't betrayed you. If you fear me leaving you for a man, that's on you. I nod, slowly understanding. She touches my cheek, my lips, and says, I love you . . . only you can trust that. Her red hair shines like an open fire, backlit by the final streams of this day's light. I promise to trust you, and love you, I say. All of you . . .

Because she is her own person, no longer the subject of my reflection, but the sovereign of her own sea. And in recognising her borders, I feel the distance between our bodies shrinking. Like we are made whole through our slippages. Our own people at the same time we spill into each other.

There are tears in her eyes. She wipes them away with the edge of the bedsheet. I want, she says quietly, to know you. I want you to lean in. Because those parts of you that feel scary to you . . . well . . . they don't feel scary to me.

I let Caragh take me in her arms, my cheek pressed hard against her naked breast. I let her hold me as I begin to sob, breath heaving. I let her run her hands through my hair. There is something in this tenderness that rewrites the story stored deep in my body, within muscle and tissue and sinew, the story that makes my body clench whenever someone raises their voice. Crying into her, so openly, so fully, and being held as gently and as resolutely as this, writes a future in which I want to live.

I want to come home, Caragh says.

limb two

On New Year's Eve, we are on the grass overlooking Bondi Beach. This edge of Sydney is heaving. People spill out of packed bars and stream down into the sea at sunset. The sky is sandy pink when Thomas puts his hand on a bee. I pull out the stinger, but the redness is already swelling into welts. In a matter of minutes, his lips are blue and I am screaming for help.

By the time the ambulance arrives, he is losing consciousness, his breath raspy, saliva gurgling in his throat. Days from now, I will learn that the word *anaphylaxis* comes from the Greek word meaning *without protection*, and it will feel like those words capture, perfectly, my grief at being hopelessly unable to protect him. Because the more I love him, the more I fear a world without him in it. In the hospital, when he opens his eyes, I think to myself, I hope I die first.

I climb into his bed moments before the clock strikes midnight, curling up beside him. His skin is shiny from the swelling, stretched wide and welted in hives. I cradle his head and whisper in his ear, Happy New Year, my love. Thomas opens one eye, half smiling. This, I promise him, is our decade. And as he closes his eye and drifts off to sleep, I tell him all the things we're going to do . . . how we're going to make beautiful babies. How he'll write his first novel, maybe more than one. How I'll get a job in publishing. How we'll be so happy. How I'm so sure of it. How I believe in it, in us, in all of it.

limb one

ON NEW YEAR'S EVE, we are still in bed at 3 pm. Greta is going through our wardrobe, pulling out everything, trying on singlets and skirts, then discarding them in exchange for dresses and trench coats. I want to look hot, she says. Caragh asks, have you heard from Maeve? Greta shakes her head. Not for a few weeks. I know she's moved in with Stella and Peggy. Caragh props herself up on her elbow and asks, how does that make you feel? Greta clutches the dress she's holding, pondering this for a moment. Then she sighs and says, I've been thinking about it a lot, and I guess I don't think healing is actually very easy when a person is just cast out and all on their own . . . I mean, I'm not saying that I want her back, or even that I want to forgive her yet, but Maeve knows that what she did was wrong. And, well, I'm glad she's got friends looking after her.

We can hear people arriving downstairs. Better get out of bed, Caragh says. Fuck the party, I say, can't we just stay here? Greta frowns. No! she says, you two are supposed to be my wing women tonight. *Fine*, I say, only half joking, and clamber out of bed to drag on a pair of jeans and a t-shirt. No way, says Caragh. This is the dawn of a new decade, we're dressing *up*! I complain that I hate new year, but then I turn around and see Caragh zipping up a pair of midnight-blue leather pants and think, actually, this isn't so bad. She grins and picks out a pair of red satin flares. Put these on, she says, throwing them at me. I oblige and she tells me I look hot, and that's all the validation I need. We decide to go topless, taping black crosses over our nipples. Greta finally decides on a pink latex dress. Caragh does Greta's make-up, then her own, while I smoke on the balcony. Caragh convinces me to put red lipstick on. Later, she says she regrets it, because the sun hasn't even gone down yet, and my lipstick is all over her face.

We live tonight in gloriously crowded hours. The party is heaving – dank heat and sweat shine. Full-throated singing. The walls of Uranian House shake as the party spills out in every direction, onto the balconies, into the yard, onto the street, into the back alley.

It's Daphne, Marg, Johnny and Geoff dancing on the dining room table.

It's Sam, Robin and Brad smoking joints in the bathtub.

It's Big Dave and Tony making out (finally!) on the kitchen bench.

It's all our friends, everyone we know, wide-eyed and belly laughing.

It's smashed wineglasses and grape-stained lips.

It's bodies everywhere, shoulder to shoulder, heart to heart.

It's Caragh cutting off her pants with a kitchen knife because the zipper is broken and she wants me to fuck her, and me, dying in hysterics.

It's all of us, sweaty and breathless, counting down 10! 9! 8! 7! 6! 5! 4! 3! 2! 1! then cheering and kissing whoever is closest.

It's me drunk crying when I remember that at the beginning of the last decade, I hated myself and was fighting just to stay. Thinking one day one day one day. I cry to Caragh, look where we are! We made it! Sobbing into her shoulder. Tears of joy and blistering relief.

It's us bursting, brilliantly, into the 1980s, full of promise and joy and unrelenting love.

It's all of us, blissfully unaware that by the end of this decade, half our home will be dead.

limb two

I MEET A woman named Giulia during orientation day for my masters. She is charismatic and charming in a way that makes me want to be in her orbit. When she invites me to have dinner with her and her friend Han one day, my body is warm and tingling.

We catch the bus to her family's restaurant in Leichhardt and sit down at a table out the front. Above us, the sky is burnt orange, making everything glow. So, says Giulia, what made you pick a masters in English Lit? Do you want to be a tortured writer, like us?

Oh no, I say, shaking my head, I want to be a publisher.

You didn't want to get an internship? she asks. That's how you get into publishing, no?

I shrug, tell her I really enjoy studying . . . I guess I also figured I could meet writers through the course. I was pretty isolated during my honours year, and I thought being back in a classroom might help me to meet people. I don't, you know, have a lot of girlfriends.

Giulia considers this, then raises her glass. Well, she says, perhaps this is the beginning of a new chapter.

In the last rays of daylight, we clink glasses and I grin at this fresh page turned over, spread wide.

Giulia notices my ring and says, are you married?

I am, yeah.

Who is he?

His name is Thomas, I say proudly. He's a writer.

Han asks, what does he write?

Short stories . . . though he's just started working on a novel.

Would he do a reading? asks Giulia. In public?

Oh, I'm not sure. Maybe?

Giulia smiles as plates of pasta are laid in front of us. She says, Han and I and a couple of other friends are putting on an open mic night in a few weeks, at a bookshop near campus. You should ask Thomas to read.

He's pretty shy, I say.

It's for emerging writers . . . Mostly uni students come, and everyone is always really supportive.

Okay, I say, I'll ask him.

As Thomas and I enter the secondhand bookshop, he turns to me and says, I've changed my mind. Can we go home?

Giulia calls my name over the gathering crowd and pushes her way through. You're here! she says. You must be Thomas. I've heard so much about you.

He blushes, suddenly sheepish. Good things, I hope.

Of course. She grins, says, we're excited to hear you read.

I nudge him and whisper in his ear, you'll be amazing.

Giulia grabs our hands and pulls us through the crowd, introducing us to other writers she knows. I repeat their names in my head to remember them, but by the time we've circled the room, they've passed through me in a blur. It astonishes me how many people Giulia knows, and how effortlessly she drifts in and out of conversations. In her presence, I feel awkward, yet drawn forward, because she carries us into connection. It makes friendship suddenly feel possible in a way neither of us imagined.

Okay, I think it's time to start, she says and leaves us for the microphone. Welcome, everyone, she says, and her voice quietens the room. I am so excited to see so many new faces here tonight. As always, we want to encourage and support each other. It is a brave and vulnerable thing to share your work in front of others, and so I hope we can recognise this and lift each other up. Now . . . who would like to go first?

To my sheer surprise and utter joy, Thomas raises his hand. He says to me, if I don't go now, I don't think I will at all.

I kiss him on the cheek, whisper, good luck, break a leg!

Great! Giulia says. Everyone, please welcome Thomas to the microphone.

There is a soft applause as Thomas weaves through the standing crowd. He stands before the microphone, opens his notebook and says, hello, I'm Thomas.

I notice that his accent becomes stronger with his nervousness, his mouth retreating to the comfort of his home tongue.

I'm going to read a section from a story I'm working on. The working title is, tree time. Thomas takes a deep breath and I lean in. He looks to me through the crowd and I give him a thumbs-up. He smiles and begins to read. Beginnings and ends aren't fixed . . . Skin is porous. Stuff seeps through the walls of time. And from within this inch-wide pocket of *now*, we slip in and out. Into the before and out into the after. Time is not a line, not a wire traversing a canyon from this ridge to that ridge. Time, I think, is the canyon, layers upon layers of earth. Red, yellow, purple. Time is circling itself like stars circle skies. Like clouds gathering, becoming wider and wider, round and around, until the present minute is rich in volume. It is a tree ring wrapping around the moment before, a trunk becoming thicker and thicker in time, so that the outer edge of now is balanced between the insides of the past and the openness of the future. This is how it feels to love you, to feel like the present is slippery, like we've been here before, over and over and over again. Because I kiss you, and it is, at once, a mere moment and an eon. And I wonder, who will remember this story? When there are no real beginnings, and no real ends. Who will remember this story?

Thomas looks up from his work, breathless and glowing. I clap first, and then I am joined by a chorus of cheers and applause.

When he is back by my side, I say, you did it! and kiss him on the mouth.

He grins, then whispers in my ear, I wrote it for you, of course.

Soon, we buy a calendar and nail it to the wall in our kitchen. With glee, we watch it fill with dinners and book launches and lunches by the water and poetry readings in friends' lounge rooms. And it feels good, becoming part of this wider circle, belonging to a conversation that breaches the walls of our own private chamber and flows outwards. For so long, Thomas and I have finished each other's sentences. Now those very sentences are routinely interrupted and challenged, cut up and rearranged. One afternoon, when Thomas resists and is backed into a corner,

Han's brother Kai tells him, if no one ever disagrees with you, Thomas, your next story will be new characters sitting in a new room discussing the same ideas you wrote about in your last one.

On the night Kai launches his poetry collection with a small press, we are drinking red wine and smoking cigarettes out the back when a woman introduces herself as Molly. She asks Han, where are you from?

Han frowns and says bluntly, Marrickville.

Molly says, oh, I mean, *where–*

Vietnam, Han interjects.

Molly proceeds to tell Han she's been to Bangkok and loved it until she was pick-pocketed on a bus.

Han does little to hide her contempt, though Molly doesn't seem to notice, continuing her long-winded stories of Bangkok until Han grabs my hand and says, my wine is empty, let's get another drink.

Inside, we top up our wines and Han says, do you think she knows Bangkok is in Thailand?

I laugh, but I feel awkward, not really knowing what to say next.

Han says, she asked me where I was from before she asked me my name.

I shrug, well you do have a bit of an accent.

Han scoffs. Thomas was standing there, too, she whips. *He* has an accent . . . why didn't she ask him where he was from?

I don't know, maybe she would have . . .

But she didn't.

I don't think she meant any offence, Han, I say.

You don't get it, she says. Like, for God's sake, I was *born here.*

Yeah, but your parents–

Han cuts me off. That woman didn't ask Thomas where he is from because Thomas is white, okay? The same reason she didn't ask *you*.

Feeling my back up, I open my mouth to speak, then hesitate, the words *you don't get it* ricocheting through me as I realise slowly, then all at once, that she's right. I don't get it, this truth I've overlooked, perhaps even evaded, ignored. Whether this was conscious or not, the end effect is the same . . . because here I am, not getting it.

Yeah, you're right, I say finally.

When people are constantly asking you where you're from, she says, the assertion they're making is that you are not from *here*.

I guess I've never had to think about it like that before, I admit. No one has ever asked me where I'm from.

You want to be a publisher, she says, you need to think about lives that aren't your own.

I ponder this for a moment, then nod. Thanks, Han . . . for explaining that.

She smiles, then clinks her glass against mine.

limb one

We are family now, Caragh says to me one morning.

'family' how soft
in the mouth, all milky fresh and
warmth dripped, and
it's not that I think otherwise, more that
I'm still searching for a word, for the
word to describe us, our house, the bar, our
street, our home, all of us in it, perhaps:
a 'comfort' of people
or a 'held' of friends
there's 'kin', of course, but maybe the better word is
'skin'?
stretching and
fleshy. skin, as in, the container, all of us
wrapped by it, all of us, milky fresh and warmth dripped,
all of us
inside it

The day Daphne is beaten, Caragh and I arrive home to red, a smear of it, across the front door of Uranian House. I think it's paint, a prank, maybe, some fuckers. But then I touch it, still wet, sticky and *warm*, and smell the rust of it on my fingertips. That's blood, says Caragh, and I feel my breath leave me, whoosh. We rush inside blood rushing up the stairs blood rushed across the tiles red Daphne's hair red Daphne's face red. Caragh screams. Daphne's body is slumped against the bath. She opens one eye, bloodshot like red cellophane. I crouch and she smiles, bruised, broken, bloodied, alive. Beaten, but heart still beating.

One day in the future, she will tell us how three men cornered her in the alleyway behind the bar when she was taking out the trash and beat her thick blue. How she had thought, the last thing I ever smell will be the stench of rot.

And it will be shocking, to hear this, but we will not find ourselves shocked.

Then she will tell us how the three men scattered like rats at the deep purr of motorbikes. How Daphne had listened to the thunderous rumble of her Guardian Angels blasting down a nearby street. How she had leant against the cold wall and closed her eyes. How she'd smiled ever so slightly, and whispered, *thank you.*

How, slowly, she climbed to her feet, adjusted her skirt, parted her blood-soaked fringe, fetched her handbag, pushed back her shoulders and walked home.

How it wasn't until she was inside Uranian House and closing the door behind her that she finally came undone.

We run Daphne a bath, bathe her, clean her, kiss her, tenderly. We hold her, love her, carry her to her bed where we wrap her in blankets and hold frozen peas to her swollen flesh. With tears in her eyes, Daphne says, you know . . . the more myself I've been, the more hostile the world around me has become. Because I look in the mirror and I see the woman I've always known myself to be, looking back at me, and though I feel strong living as I am, walking down the street and catching my reflection in a shop window and feeling a kick of excitement – euphoria even – at the woman I see, I feel like I have a thinner skin now . . . like the world has worn this tree down to paper, so that the insults and the punches just tear straight through me. And in those moments, all the horrible things people say about me . . . well, I guess I believe them.

People often talk about how what doesn't kill you makes you stronger. And I think, sometimes, what doesn't kill you makes you tired.

We take Daphne in our arms and tell her she is beautiful. We tell her she is loved. We remind her of all the good things, her laugh, her generosity, her tenacity, her humour. Because the good things have been beaten small. We make the good things feel big, so big that she becomes swollen, too, with goodness. So that her heart feels heavy, not with hate, but with bright pink love. We tell these truths until she believes us once more. Until she's laughing at Caragh's attempt to sing a lullaby, and we shake, giggling, and then we cry for her, cry for us, for our family, our queerness, our joy that is so often and so readily beaten.

I fetch my notebook. It's raining outside, now, small footprints of sky on the windowpane. I read Caragh and Daphne my poem, and when I'm done, they smile together in the gentle quiet. Skin, she says. Holding Daphne's hand, holding Caragh's hand, I nod. Yeah, we are . . . we are skin.

limb two

MORGAN IS DIAGNOSED with, *it's like cancer*, except it's not cancer, Gwen tells Thomas. I am lying in our bed, listening to him in the kitchen talking to his mother on the phone.

What do you mean, it's *like* cancer?

How can they not know?

Okay, okay, Mam, I'm sorry.

Yes, I know it's scary.

When will you go?

Are you sure?

Okay, if it's what you both want.

Thomas hangs up the phone and wanders over, gets back into bed, curls up, becomes smaller, shoulders rolling in, knees tucked. Then, in a very quiet voice, he looks up at me and says, Mam says my tad is sick. They want to go back to Wales.

We should go with them, I say.

Thomas shakes his head, no, no. You need to finish your studies.

That can wait.

No, he says. And he looks as if he's about to say something else, but he hesitates, swallowing the words. He half smiles, then pulls the sheet over his head. I kiss the small of his body through the cotton.

Giulia and I meet Kai at Central Station and catch the train to Newtown. The air on King Street is damp and heavy with the promise of a storm, the sky gathering itself, holding its breath, becoming rich with darkness. Thomas is already at the restaurant when we arrive. He gives me a glass of wine and I ask, what are you reading?

You haven't heard it yet, he says. I've only just started working on it.

I'm excited then, I say.

He takes a sip of his wine and turns away, eyeing the gathering crowd.

Han walks in, into the warm glow of the restaurant and takes off her winter coat and scarf. Gosh it's cold out there, she says.

Nice to see you, I say as she embraces me.

You too, she says. Hi, Thomas.

Hello, he says quietly, his eyes milky, mind elsewhere.

Giulia hands Han a glass of wine. Thanks, she says, and kisses Giulia's cheeks. Are you reading?

Giulia grins. Yeah, a poem I think . . .Thomas, are you reading tonight?

He nods absentmindedly, whispers something under his breath, which none of us hear, an afterthought maybe, then leaves the conversation, wandering over to a table where two of Kai's friends are selling zines.

Han gently pulls me close and asks, is Thomas okay?

I whisper in her ear, his dad is sick.

With what?

I shrug. It's like, some sort of cancer . . .

Oh, she says. Poor Thomas.

But it's not cancer, I say.

Giulia frowns. What is it then?

They're not sure, really.

Han shakes her head, says, that's really tough.

I nod and take a sip of my wine. His parents are moving back to Wales.

Will he go with them?

I said that we should go, but he doesn't want to. He wants to stay until I finish my masters.

Well, we only have one term left, Giulia says, hopefully you can go after that. I chose not to go back to Italy when my nona died, and I've always regretted it . . . Anyway, we're here for you. Lean on us if you need to.

I will, I say. And please don't say anything to Thomas. You know how private he is.

We won't, Han promises.

Tuesdays here have become a staple for us. The restaurant, with its beige walls and red wood furnishings, is closed for dining on Tuesday nights, opening instead for readings and wine. In the soft glow of vintage light fixtures, our friends share their words and we are both shaken and soothed. We hold our breath as the reader lures our bodies into a vortex of stress, exhaling in a rush when they let go, releasing us to ourselves. That, Han will say, is the purpose of art. It's all about tension and relief.

The purpose of story, Kai will say as he pours another glass of wine, is to remember. And when Giulia asks what he means by this, he will tell the story of an ancient god who was dismembered, his body thrown all around the world. To remember is to *re-member* the dis-membered body, some truth you forgot when you were blown apart. Storytelling is the act of piecing you back together.

We have warm bara brith with a pot of tea in Gwen and Morgan's living room. Their belongings are packed up in boxes stacked against the wall, ready for the removalists. Gwen wipes Morgan's chin with a tissue and says, you'll feel better when you're home.

Thomas blows on his tea, saying nothing.

I reach into my handbag and pull out a wrapped gift. I hand it to Gwen and say, for the plane.

She smiles, unwraps the book, and reads the title aloud, *An Open Swimmer.*

It's by a young author from Western Australia, I say, Tim Winton . . . The book just won the Vogel Award.

Thomas looks up from his tea. I pinch his cheek and say, he's a beautiful writer. Just like you.

Thank you, Gwen says, reaching for my hand, squeezing it gently, small tears in her eyes. Visit us, please.

Thomas steps up to the microphone. Noswaith dda, he says. These words mean good evening in my mother's tongue, in my father's tongue, soft in my mouth, like a tea brewed from the flowers of my nain's garden . . .

Thomas pauses, looks out and his watery gaze meets mine.

There is another word . . . *hiraeth* . . . in my mother's tongue, in my father's tongue, soft in my mouth, that I can't tell you . . . even though I want to . . . kiss you . . . I cannot give you hiraeth and take a word from your mouth . . . because no such word exists. I could tell you it's a deep craving for home. That *hiraeth* means longing, nostalgia, yearning. But this is not *enough* . . . I could tell you hiraeth is for the mountains, for the valleys, for the streams . . . for ashen skies and broken ocean. But this is not *enough* . . . because hiraeth is in the sweep of black tide over smooth black stone. In the feathers of seabirds strewn along the shore, storm wet and glistening. Hiraeth is in the scream of the gale and the song of the stream, all frothy and bubbling and green. Hiraeth is in the stillness of crushed snow on the crest of Snowdonia, in the weight and the thaw and the flow down into spring. Hiraeth is in the sheer drop of cracked cliff into ocean, in the jagged burnt umber and the wind chopped grey. Hiraeth is in the slow caress of summer grass and the dusk pink drifting in over the North Sea. And so, I close my eyes and swallow hiraeth, feel its longing in my throat, feel its ache in my belly, and wonder, what will a writer say to his lover of love and pain, in the soft absence of a word?

limb one

IT BEGINS AS an abstraction. A disembodied rumour, imperceptible to the touch, passed around sand dunes and alleyways.

It's a cancer that *only* kills gays.
You can't *catch* cancer, I say.

I don't remember the specifics of its beginning, because at first it is so unbelievable and so far-flung, it feels, to us, like a ghost story, one you'd tell around a campfire to scare your friends. Boo!

We can't yet see that this ghost story will become a story of ghosts. Because the rumour has no legs, no body, until it becomes a corpse.

Sam dies in St Vincent's Hospital before they have a name for the sickness that has turned his skin translucent. It all happens so quickly. In a matter of weeks, our friend who gets a cough and makes a joke about how he's smoked one too many joints in our bathtub, dies. In a hospital bed with deep sunken cheeks, Sam exhales, and all that made him our hilariously self-deprecating, hopelessly loving Sam escapes his throat and passes out between his teeth.

Come on, Caragh whispers. Let's give her some space . . . I nod and leave the room with Johnny, Caragh and Dave, turning at the last moment to see Daphne gently closing Sam's eyes. I'll never not love you, she says.

In the hallway, I ask Caragh, did you know? Caragh nods. I mean, not from Daphne or Sam, but I always thought it, she says. I lean my head back against the wall, feel it smooth and glossy. I tell Caragh I love how observant she is. How much I admire her. I love you, I say, trying not to imagine what it would feel like to be in there, closing her eyes.

A swarm of nurses hurries down the hallway with buckets and mops. Johnny says, hey, please, just wait a minute . . . but they barge past, flooding into Sam's room. Daphne is pushed out of the way, out of the room, into the hallway, where she sighs and says quietly, he's gone, isn't he? Yes, hon, says Johnny. Sam is gone.

Intrigue and suspicion have transformed into terror, because Sam is taken at thirty-one, and suddenly the rumour has legs.

Suddenly, the rumour is a curse, whispered between bedsheets: *you're next.*

It's a death sentence, they say. No one survives.

limb two

For a while, Morgan gets better. We get a call every Sunday night and Gwen tells us how the sea air has cleansed his lungs, how the pink has returned to his skin, how home has healed his heart. Thomas, for this time, is once again part of the conversation. When we're at the pub or down by the water with our friends he is laughing with us, sharing stories, offering his opinion. I feel relieved to find him at his desk writing, to kiss him and feel him kiss me back. His eyes are no longer opaque with distant thoughts, but clear as daylight. Thomas is right here, with me. Until one Sunday, he picks up the phone, and I see him fold slowly in two.

I hand in my thesis this week, I remind him. We should go.

He asks the very real *hows* of uprooting our lives. *How* will we pay for the tickets? *How* will we keep the apartment? *How* long will we even go for? Questions I can't answer. Still, I promise him, we'll make it work.

We exhale sighs of relief when Kai's friend Angie agrees to take over our lease. I tell her, it's worth it for how cheap the rent is . . . Still, I'd be careful walking home after dark, especially if you're on your own.

She frowns, says, I'm not worried about the neighbourhood.

There's just some real low-lifes around, like I wouldn't–

Angie cuts me off. I said, I'm not worried.

Thomas and I buy our tickets with the money Angie gives us for the bond and our kitchen appliances. Whatever she doesn't want, Thomas sells for cash. When I learn he sold his typewriter, too, I go down to the pawn shop to buy it back, but find that it's already been sold. Thomas says, you're being too sentimental. And anyway, I couldn't have taken it on the plane.

I don't want you to stop writing, I say.

I'll buy one over there.

My parents come down from Newcastle to drive us to the airport. Mum sobs quietly in the front passenger seat all the way to the drop-off outside the terminal. It's okay, Mum, I say, we'll be back.

Promise me?

Yes, of course. I promise.

I've never been on a plane. We take off and I watch everything I've ever known shrink, so that the whole of the Hawkesbury River becomes a thin blue vein. The great stretch of earth between the home I grew up in and the home I've just left narrows as we climb higher and higher, until there's barely a gap, and my limbs are made shaky by sickening nerves. So much so that for the first few hours, I sit, unable to read, unable to think of anything but the overwhelming height of it all.

Lunch is served in plastic containers. The meal steams when I remove the foil lid. I turn away from the window, use the food as a distraction from the sky outside and spoon small squares of mashed potato and gelatinous lamb stew into my mouth. When I've mopped up the last of the juices with my bread roll, Thomas asks if I want him to read to me.

I close my eyes, whisper, yes, please.

– I go to the bathroom and hike up my skirt to pull down my stockings – in the thin mirror I catch sight of my belly – the huge round of it – skin stretched pale white – my belly is marbled by blue vein – I stare down at it – smooth my palm around its wide curve – I feel my heart slow – I look up into the mirror and see her standing behind me – she wraps her arms around my body – her hands cradling the full of my pregnancy – I see her nestle her face into the shallow of my neck – kiss the corner of my jaw –

I wake in a yelp of dry breath to find myself back in my seat, buckled in. Thomas is asleep beside me, book open on his lap, head resting gently on my shoulder. Just a dream, I whisper, just a dream. Just a dream. Just a dream.

I don't sleep during the second leg, fearful of what I might dream. I just read until my eyes become sandpaper sore. When we begin our descent over London, I feel wired awake by my own sleep deprivation, like I'm walking on borrowed time as we move through the terminal, showing our passports, collecting our bags. As we step out of the terminal the cold bites at our exposed ankles and wrists, at the backs of our necks. It bites at our faces. It makes everything feel urgent.

We catch the train into London, and then board a bus for Cardiff. I slump against the glass, Thomas asleep again in the seat beside me. I peer out as brick terraces give way to standalone cottages, as backyards give way to rolling hills. The world outside passes in a blur of grey and pale green. Everything here feels smaller and more contained, neat paddocks bordered by stone walls. Trees, spindly and leafless. Even the sky is low-hanging, shrouding the earth like a woollen blanket. It is so unlike the wide stretches of sunburnt bush and huge, towering skies, all I've ever known. And yet, something here feels old, and strangely familiar. As we drive closer to the border of Wales, this feeling only intensifies, so much so that when we meet Gwen at the bus station in Cardiff and get into her sparrow-blue Mini Cooper for our final leg of the journey, out to the ragged coast of northwest Wales, I feel as if my body is being repeated in the landscape, or as if the landscape is repeated in me. We wind through mountains of exposed rock and patched snow, until huge cracked cliffs fall away to windswept ocean, and I experience a bizarre feeling of returning somewhere I've never been, like my body is remembering. I tell Thomas, I feel like I've been here before.

He turns around in his seat, says, you have, in my stories.

No, I say, not like that. It's like I've *been* here before.

Do you know where your family is from, love? asks Gwen from the driver's seat.

I meet her gaze in the rearview mirror and shake my head. I know we've been in Australia for several generations, I say. I thought we came from England, but my parents have never spoken about our family tree.

Thomas is grinning. He says over his shoulder, maybe you're a Welshwoman deep down . . . a Cymraes.

We pull up a pebbly driveway in front of a white-clad cottage with a thatched roof. The front door is pale blue and so small Thomas has to duck his head to walk through it. Inside, a pot-belly fire is burning. Morgan is sitting in an armchair in front of the fire, wrapped in a blanket, with a beanie on and a scarf around his neck. At the sight of him, I let go of my bag, dropping it at my feet. His cheeks are sunken, all hollowed out. On the bridge of his nose and around his mouth are dark lesions. They're oddly shaped, like red bruises. Look who's here, says Gwen. They've come all this way . . . I told them not to, of course, but they insisted. They wanted to see you, Morgan.

Thomas puts his bag down and treads lightly towards his father. Hi, Tad, he says.

Morgan looks up at his son, his eyes yellow-glazed and tired. Thomas, he whispers. Then he asks something I can't make out, and Thomas, kneeling beside him, answers in Welsh.

You look exhausted, Gwen says to me, picking up my bag. Let me show you to where you're sleeping.

She guides me down a narrow hallway, into a small room with a low ceiling. There is a double bed, neatly made with tucked sheets and a quilt that has ruffled edges. At the foot of the bed are two folded towels and a bar of pink soap. I pull apart lace curtains and peer out into the garden, to rosebushes bordered by a weathered picket fence. Beyond, tufts of windswept grass give way to a pebbly beach, strewn with blackened seaweed, driftwood and feathers. Beyond, the Atlantic Ocean, its surface green and frilled.

Gwen puts my bag down beside the armchair in the corner of the bedroom. Make yourself at home, she says.

I wake in the early hours of the morning. It's still dark out, the ocean roaring through soupy blackness. I try to go back to sleep, but the wash of water over pebbles keeps me here. *So this is jetlag,* I think to myself, finding a strange joy in the novelty of being wide awake at this hour, of everything being flipped back to front and my body scrambling to adapt.

I go out into the kitchen to get some water. The logs in the potbelly are still smouldering, making the room lemony and warm. I am at the tap filling up a glass when Gwen walks out in a robe and slippers. Oh! she yelps when she sees me. You scared the living daylights out of me.

Sorry, Gwen, I say, and turn off the tap.

She smiles, says, never you mind. Then she touches her cool palm to my face, cradling my cheek. It's nice to have you here, it really is.

limb one

DAPHNE PUTS ON her favourite sequined dress. She's wearing shark-blue eye shadow and lashes. Johnny tells her not to wear so much make-up to a funeral. She says, my grief will run as art.

We bury a friend – Sam.

The sun is cracked confetti on the sea beyond as Sam's coffin is lowered into a plot at Waverley. We wrote to Sam's father to tell him of his son's death, but the man never replied. Silence, we are already learning, will be the overwhelming and recurrent quality of this decade and the next.

We remember his singing, red wine-stained lips. We remember his Sunday afternoons on the piano, cigarette hanging from his mouth, hands gliding across the keys as we danced our bodies around him. We remember the time he tried stand-up at the bar and how it turned into a rude roast of everyone he loved. How we laughed anyway. How we loved him.

Daphne says, loving you was like opening the windows to let the sunshine in. Because, in a world that tells me so often that I should not exist, you made everything worth existing for. Despite all the hardness forced upon us, your love kept me soft. I am beautifully soft, thanks to your tenderness and your care. And I will remain soft, for you, in your absence. I will enjoy lightly and dance gently and laugh often and remember you fondly. Until we meet again.

Back at home, I sit with Dave sharing a cigarette and drinking beer beneath the ivy in the backyard in soft, blue light. Everyone else is inside, with Daphne, listening to Sam's favourite record. Dave asks me, did Johnny tell you I saw my kids? I reply, surprised, *what*? No! Dave nods. Yeah, he says. Andy and Emma. I was down by the David Jones on Elizabeth Street, and I saw them getting onto a bus. Dave's voice breaks and his eyes swell with tears as he says, I recognised Emma immediately, but Andy was just a kid when Christine threw me out, and, well . . . it took me a minute to realise who he was. I even thought to myself, who's that boy she's with? Dave laughs now. I thought, does my little girl have a boyfriend? And then it hit me. I didn't recognise my own son.

Putting my arm around Dave, he leans into me, resting his tired head on my shoulder. I used to take them every year when they were kids to see those Christmas window displays . . . I reckon that's what they were doing there . . . or at least, I'd like to think they were, that they still go . . . that they still remember me taking them there . . . I squeeze Dave's shoulder and tell him, they'd remember. And I reckon they'd remember you fondly. Dave begins to sob. I squeeze him again and say, you know, you'll always be their dad . . . Dave shudders as he says, quieter now, I'm always wondering what horrible things Christine would have told them about me . . . Hey, I say, you can't think like that. He shakes his head. She screamed at me the day my name got published. Said I was sick in the head. Perverted . . . yeah, that's the word she used. Just kept screaming it, over and over . . . I catch Dave's tears with my sleeve. Above us, bats fly through the cool sky of dusk. I tell him, love isn't just a word we say. It's *felt* . . . And wherever your kids are, they'll always be able to feel how much you love them. You remember that, okay? Dave smiles now, beneath the stars appearing. He says, Tony's asked me to move in with him. I grin. That's wonderful! He laughs, says, I know . . . I really love him. Then he whispers, it's a lot, isn't it? The price we pay for this love.

Later, upstairs and naked in our bed, I ask Caragh, do you think, when we die, that we meet our loves again? A beeswax candle is burning in a jar on my desk. It smells of sandalwood and rose. In the dancing light of the candle, Caragh sighs and says, I hope not. I frown, what do you mean you *hope not*? Caragh rolls onto her side to face me. Well, if I die and you're still here, I hope that you would love again . . . as fully and wholeheartedly as you love me right now. And I guess I just don't know if you would commit yourself to loving again if you thought you and I were going to find each other in death. Caragh takes a deep breath and says, think of Marg. She was barely thirty when Ruby died. And

I get it, when she says that Ruby was her soul love. I understand and respect her resoluteness. But there's also a part of me that feels sad imagining you closing yourself off like that.

I am lying on my back when she says this. I stare up at the paper notes we've tacked to the ceiling above our bed and feel my head spinning. She puts her hand on the flat between my breasts. I swallow her words and feel them, sharp in my throat. Are you okay? she asks. I shake my head and tell her, I just keep thinking . . . even if we were to live to one hundred, that still feels like such a grossly inadequate amount of time. Caragh kisses me on the mouth. I think we are lucky, she says, to feel like there isn't *enough* time.

limb two

THOMAS AND I go to the pub for roast lunch on Sunday. We take Gwen's Mini, Thomas driving down the coast road. He tells me, the cottage was my grandparents', but they both passed when I was ten. Within a week of each other, after thirty-eight years together . . . My nain had been sick for a long time, she died slowly. I remember her death seemed to drag on and on. It was so painful for my mam. Then the day before we buried her, my taid just dropped dead. Can you believe it? Mam said he died of a broken heart.

I'm gazing out the window, at the huge green hills that give way suddenly to ocean, my head resting against the glass. I say, yeah, I'd believe that.

He touches my hand and I turn my head to face him. Thomas looks as if he's about to say something, but he holds the words back and offers instead a quiet smile.

Is that when you left for Australia?

He nods. My mam was really depressed after they passed. She never had any sisters or brothers, so she felt really alone without them. I think Tad thought moving to Australia could be the beginning of a new life for her, that it would save her . . . Everyone in the village thought he was absolutely mad. But it did, save her, I think. She was really happy there. Funny now that they're back here, you know, that Mam thought returning could be a way to save *him*.

It still might, I say . . . save him.

Thomas goes quiet now, focusing ahead as we turn a corner and drive down a cobblestoned high street, lined by fishermen's cottages and quaint shop windows. There's a sweets shop, a fishmonger, a bakery, and a pub on the corner which overlooks a small cove that opens to the sea. Thomas points to a cottage painted baby blue with white detailing around the windows. That was the house I grew up in, he says. We sold it when we moved.

It's really cute, I say as he pulls in to the kerb in front of the bakery. We get out and run through thin rain into the pub. Inside, in the cosy warmth of an open fire, locals are gathered around wooden tables or standing around the bar. Clumps of holly are arranged between lit candles along the mantle above the fireplace, and there's Christmas tinsel strung along the countertop. The room smells of tobacco and mulled wine.

As we enter, the entire pub quietens, hushed until everyone is completely silent and staring at us. Thomas grabs my hand and walks between tables to the bar where he greets a balding man with a thick white beard. His pale skin is flushed pink around his neck and cheeks. Towel-drying a glass, he looks at us, suspiciously, until Thomas says his name, Thomas Bateman. And then begins speaking to the man in Welsh.

The barman shouts, Thomas Bateman! Then cracks a wide grin, his eyes disappearing between deep wrinkles. He belly laughs and responds to Thomas in Welsh. Then he puts down the glass, slings the tea towel over his shoulder and lunges across the bar to embrace Thomas. A few locals standing around the bar grin and nod to acknowledge us, and everyone goes back to their conversations.

Well, bugger me, says another man clutching a pint of beer. I was only talking about you with your mam last week.

Thomas introduces the man behind the bar as Bryn, and the one beside me as Hari. He says, they were in high school with my tad.

Bryn says, not just that! I was best man at his wedding. Can't forget that!

Thomas smiles, says, of course not, Bryn. Then he introduces me to both of them.

I didn't believe your mam, you know, says Hari. When she said you got married. I thought, no, not little Thomas from down the road. Snotty little Thomas. Don't you go telling me he's got a wife!

Bryn laughs. And I suppose you drink beer now, too, eh?

Hari says, fuck we're getting on now, ay Bryn.

Bryn shakes his head, speak for yourself, now Hari! I'm barely a day over thirty.

Ha! Hari shouts, slamming his beer down on the countertop, froth spilling over its lip. You can't trick a tricker, Bryn.

Bryn chucks the tea towel to Hari to mop up the spilt beer, then says in a softer voice, how is old Morgan now anyway?

Ah . . . Thomas hesitates, though I'm not sure why.

He was coming in here, looking great, we all thought. Couldn't even tell he'd been sick. But your mam said he's taken a turn now, poor Morgan.

Hari adds, we're all worried about him.

He's getting better, says Thomas. I'd say he might even make it here on Christmas Eve.

Ah, good, says Hari, patting Thomas on the shoulder. That's what we like to hear. Then he turns to me and says, Christmas Eve is the night of nights. The whole village is in 'ere. Packed like sardines in a tin.

I grin and tell him, well I look forward to it.

limb one

Geoff gets sick and goes to hospital. He's finding it hard to breathe, says it feels like he's breathing through mesh. We all hold our breath.

There is a howling in the bathroom. I pull the shower curtain back and find Johnny sitting in an empty bath, fully clothed. His face is a red mess of tears and snot, his eyes bloodshot. I crouch down beside him and say, Geoff is going to be okay. They can treat a chest infection . . . he's going to be okay. Johnny shakes his head. Geoff has it, he says, and I feel my blood run cold. I ask him, what do you mean? Johnny . . . How can he?

We know now that AIDS is passed through bodily fluids. We know now that the fucking and the lovemaking and the pleasure chasing is how it spreads. We know now that it gets in through our joy and kills us. It's a gay disease, the newspapers say, the radio says, the television says. And all these lovers who just want to be held are made dead by the very thing that makes them feel alive.

How cruel is it, I cry to Caragh, that all those people who have called us dirty and disease-ridden for so long finally have a leg to stand on. AIDS is just affirming for them that they've been right about us all along. Caragh holds me in her arms. I know, she says, I know . . . And then she is crying, too, because all the shame the world has imposed upon us and instilled within us rears its filthy head with startling intensity. We feel it so acutely. It makes us want to die.

I fucked someone else, Johnny manages to say between heavy sobs. And now he's going to die. I . . . I . . . I've killed him. Johnny is hysterical now, screaming. I've killed the love of my life!

Caragh and I go to the hospital to spend the afternoon with Geoff. We take him a thermos of black coffee and a work we've made together to stand on his bedside table. It is a painting of tiny bodies in billowing dresses floating between pink clouds. The text in the centre reads,

> *I will find you, in this wide river in the sky,*
> *and we will dance and swim*

Geoff tells us he loves it and thanks us, then he looks down into his lap and says, it's not a chest infection. And I watch Caragh's eyes glass over. Geoff tells us how they're not going to try treatment, because they don't think his body is strong enough. I think we know, he says, how this story ends. Caragh breaks into loud cries, burying her face into his thin chest bone. I feel like I have gravel in my throat. It makes it all so hard to swallow. I want to see Johnny, he says. I need to tell him it's okay, that I forgive him.

Caragh and I drink wine and smoke cigarettes on our balcony in our underwear. The air is laden. Summer is ringing in the wild chorus of cicadas. A Christmas beetle crawls along the balcony railing. I take a deep drag of my cigarette. My fingertips are shaking, slightly. I exhale and tell her, I am so fucking mad. Caragh says, I know . . . And I think it's okay to feel everything you're feeling, but you have to remember no one is simply good or simply bad. I take another drag of my cigarette, exhale with force and tell her, you know, they promised each other they'd be exclusive, at least for the time being, in the hope they might escape it . . . Caragh looks to me and says, I know, Marg told me. I shake my head. I think I've just lost all respect. Caragh swirls her wine in her glass, takes a sip and swallows. People don't need to be righteous in order to be respected, she says. And after a long pause, I ask her, can you forgive Johnny? She takes hold of my hand and says, Geoff already has.

Geoff returns from the hospital and Johnny sets up a bed in the living room so that we can all be around him. I learn through observing them with each other that there is grace in letting go. That forgiveness is its own way of coming home.

Johnny comes into our room when we are working together and sits down beside us. He looks down at the canvas, at the multiple limbs extending from a mask in the centre of the painting. The text reads,

wear a mask for long enough
it may become your face

Is this for your show? he asks. Yes, Caragh says proudly, it's going to be a masquerade. She passes him a collage produced by Claude Cahun and Marcel Moore sometime in the 1930s. This, she says, is informing our body of work. I add, it's about the masks we adorn, as people, but also as gendered bodies. Caragh says, the whole world is a stage. And we are all performers. Daphne, who is sitting on our balcony smoking a joint, chimes in. Hey! she says, I told you that! Johnny says, well as Geoff likes to tell me, the best poets steal. To this, Daphne throws her head back and laughs, full throat cackle. Johnny grins. I'm so proud of you both. Remember me, please, when you're famous? We laugh, though inside we're glowing, because he's right, getting representation with a gallery as commercial as Bart's is everything we've ever dreamt of. Everyone knows our solo show is going to make us stars.

Johnny asks, when is the opening? Next year, I say, in August. Johnny smiles, but his expression trembles. I wish Geoff could see it . . . he has always been your biggest champion. Caragh wipes a stray tear from Johnny's cheek. We know, she whispers. Johnny clears his throat, then says, I actually came in here because I need your help . . . You know I despise weddings, them being a great big hoo-ha for the straights and all, but Geoff has always wanted one. And so, I thought, we should have a wedding. I want to surprise him . . . in the backyard, with everyone we love. Will you help me?

limb two

HARI AND BRYN drop by the day before Christmas Eve. Owain, the village doctor, is tending to Morgan in the living room when they walk in. Bryn knocks as he enters, and is in the cottage before Gwen can get to the door. The surly men blow in like a roll cloud, engulfing the space. I am sitting on the couch opposite Morgan, nursing a mug of hot coffee when they enter. I watch their faces change shape, shock and horror warping their mouths as they take in the sight of Morgan. Gwen stands in the way, as if to block out what they've already seen. But she can't take the image back.

There is a long and uncomfortable silence, broken when Bryn says, well, bloody hell, now, Morgan. You've seen better days.

Morgan, slumped in his chair, grins at this. He laughs. The sound is raspy but clotted with unadulterated delight.

We brought you this, Hari says. He is speaking very loudly and enunciating every word. It's a leg of smoked ham, it is.

He might be sick, Hari, says Owain with a cheeky grin, but he can still hear ya.

Hari says, oh. Then cracks up.

Owain stands up from where he's kneeling on the floor, wraps his stethoscope around his neck and walks over to greet Hari and Bryn. The men embrace. It's good to see you, says Owain.

Merry Christmas, says Bryn.

Hari turns to me and says, we was all at school together. Us four. Can you imagine?

Bryn laughs. Ceg fawr oeddech chi!

I must be looking wide-eyed with confusion, because Bryn notices and apologises. Sorry, love. What I said was, big mouths we were. Gave our teacher a right old headache!

Gwen whips, that's if you ever went to class!

Ah, come on, now, Gwen! croaks Morgan from his chair.

My mam always said I fancied the naughty boys, she teases.

Morgan playfully reaches his hand out and taps her on the bum.

Thomas looks at me, visibly mortified by his parents flirting with each other. I grin at this, at the loud racket in the room, at the heartiness of it all. This moment, split open like an oyster, warm brine flowing out, tastes joyous.

Bryn, Owain and Hari are still here drinking whiskey by the fire with Morgan when there's another knock at the door. Gwen opens it to a man and woman, who walk in holding hands.

Thomas, sitting at the kitchen bench with me, whispers in my ear, that's my uncle, Aeron. He's my tad's younger brother. And that's his wife, Heledd. They live in her family's village about an hour south of here.

Gwen welcomes them in. Aeron, you remember Bryn and Hari and Owain?

Aeron nods silently, staring at Morgan.

This is Heledd, Gwen says, and turns to Owain. She's a doctor, like you.

Owain nods. I remember. Nice to see you both.

Gwen turns back to Heledd and says, Owain's been taking such good care of my Morgan.

Aeron smiles gently and says something to Morgan in Welsh, then moves towards his brother, perhaps for a hug, but Heledd pulls on his hand, holding him back.

His face, she says to Gwen.

Yes, it's the cancer, she says.

Heledd shakes her head, no, she says, I've seen this–

Gwen cuts her off. Says, yes, well you're a doctor, Heledd, I'm sure you've seen cancer before. Then she abruptly changes the topic. How's your room at the pub?

Fine, says Heledd.

I'm sorry we didn't have the room for you to stay here, says Gwen.

No, says Heledd, I think it's a good thing we're not.

I look to Thomas, confused by the tension between these two women, hoping for an answer, but he looks as at sea as I am.

Thomas, says Gwen, say helo to your Wncl a Anti.

Hi, he says, getting up from the bench to greet them.

Whoa, Aeron exclaims, his face now lighting up. Look at you! Taller than me, you are.

Thomas, suddenly blushed and sheepish, hugs his uncle, and then his aunt. You alright? he says to Heledd as he embraces her.

Yes, we're good, she responds.

Gwen motions with her hand for me to come over. She introduces me, and I hug Aeron and Heledd.

Right, says Heledd, we best be getting off. We just popped on in to let you know we've arrived.

Gwen says, yes, don't want to be driving in the dark.

See you on Christmas. We'll come around half ten?

We'll see you tomorrow, Heledd, says Gwen. We always go to the pub at Christmas Eve.

Best night of the year, it is! shouts Hari from the couch.

Heledd says in a hushed tone, you can't be bringing him to the pub, Gwen.

He'll be fine, snaps Gwen.

It's not *him* I'm worried about.

To this, Gwen opens the door. Right then, she says, see you tomorrow.

Heledd and Aeron walk out and Gwen closes the door behind them. She turns to the room and asks, another drink?

Hari eyes his near-empty glass and says, sure, Gwen. Just a small one, thanks.

Bryn nods, says, a nightcap. Thanks, Gwen.

I watch Gwen go to the drinks cabinet to fetch the whiskey. She's tense, her shoulders held high up around her neck, her lips pursed, eyes focused, as if her inner monologue is saying, just this, just *do this*, Gwen. And I wonder, what is she carrying? What is making her breath so short and shallow?

Mam, Thomas says quietly, his voice quivering with uncertainty. What was Heledd saying that for?

Owain? Gwen says, ignoring her son. Another pour?

Owain says, sure. Thanks, Gwen.

What did she mean, Mam?

Gwen looks at Thomas, then to Owain, searching.

Owain says, not to worry, Thomas. Not everyone in medicine agrees all the time . . . and some doctors have strong views about how to treat your tad's illness.

The cancer?

Yes, says Owain kindly, the cancer.

Thomas and I go for a walk along the beach and up a path that leads to the headland. The wind is so strong at the top of the hill that we spread our jackets like wings and lean against it. The force of the gusts is enough to stop us falling forward, enough to defy gravity. We are laughing and squealing like children, as if the sheer power of the wind has stripped entire years from our bodies. Thomas shouts into the sky, Ahhhhh!!!

When we get back to the cottage, we have a bath together, thawing out the cold. Thomas says, thank you for being here with me. I know it isn't easy, but I'm grateful you're here.

We help Gwen get Morgan into the front passenger seat of the Mini, then jump in the back. We're all dressed up in our best clothes. As we drive down the coast road towards the village, the clouds pull apart over the ocean and rays of sunshine beam down in huge pillars of gold light. Wow, Gwen says, would you look at that.

In the rearview mirror, I see the edge of Morgan's mouth, smiling.

Gwen parks in front of the sweets shop. The whole of the high street is lined with parked cars and there are bicycles stacked outside the pub. Thomas slings Morgan's arm over his shoulder to help his tad down the sidewalk, Gwen and I walking a little ahead.

Gwen holds the door open for us to enter. I see Heledd and Aeron over by the fire, sitting in armchairs drinking and chatting to another couple. Thomas walks through with his tad and people turn as they pass, becoming quiet at the sight of Morgan. He's wrapped up with a beanie, scarf and thick jacket, but his face is exposed for everyone to see. Stepping into the glow of the fire, his lesions glisten like black pudding. I see Heledd, scowling.

Hushed murmurs are passed around the room.

Bryn, behind the bar, calls out, ay, Morgan! What you drinking?

But before Morgan can respond, the woman sitting with Heledd stands up. She says something in Welsh that makes people gasp.

She's right, says another woman, I seen that on TV.

Gwen, eyes glassing over, says, that's none of your business!

It is, the woman snaps, *our* business if you're bringing him in 'ere. We could catch it!

I feel a strange surge of panic and reach for Thomas's hand. He grips mine and squeezes it so hard it hurts.

Bryn turns off the Christmas carols playing through the radio. Alright, if you're worried about my friend 'ere, you can leave, he says. Now.

I watch in horror as people all around the bar whisper to each other, put down their drinks, grab their handbags and jackets, and walk out, one by one until there's only ten or so people left in the pub.

Bryn, still standing tall, smiles at Morgan. He turns the music back on. Okay, says Bryn, well, now we can get on and enjoy ourselves. Who wants a drink?

limb one

HE WANTED TO go to Greece, Johnny tells us. Caragh smiles.
I know how to take him there.

We buy tubes of Prussian Blue, Salmon Gum and Titanium White,
and a wide piece of canvas. Tony asks us, what's this for? We're
painting a backdrop to the altar, I say. Tony smiles. Here, he says
as he closes the cash register drawer, passing us our paints, these
are on me. Caragh frowns, says, no, that's too much! Tony shakes
his head. Consider it my wedding gift. I touch his hand over the
counter, squeezing it gently. See you there, I say. Tony kisses my
hand. I wouldn't miss it for the world.

Caragh and I string up the canvas across the back fence,
stretched taut like skin. In the dying light, we set up a stage
light we've borrowed from Daphne and angle it towards the
blank canvas. Johnny brings out two plates of gnocchi and
a bottle of shiraz, lays them on the outdoor table. He lights

a cigarette, watching us mix paints. No, no, no, says Caragh, waving her hand in front of him. Turn around and go inside! He laughs, oh, come on! You know I hate surprises. We spin him around and gently nudge him back towards the house. Johnny throws his hands up theatrically. Fine! he says as he walks up the back steps, turning in the doorway, finger pointed back at us. It better be good!

We fork gnocchi into each other's mouths as the sky becomes watery black above us. When we're finished, Caragh unscrews the bottle and pours us each a glass. You ready? she asks. I eye off the stretch of white canvas, almost as wide as the courtyard. It's going to be a long night, I say as I lean in to kiss her. She grins, better get started then.

Sometimes I think, I cannot love her more. But then I see her put down her paintbrush and scoop up a wad of paint with her hand, turn to the canvas, and flesh out an ocean with her palm, and I feel the edge of my love expanding. Because loving her is a process of learning her. It is walking through a landscape to a horizon that deepens the closer I get. It is all the parts of her that were once tinged blue with distance, now here, close up, learnt and full of colour. It is me, giddy with excitement at seeing another formation take shape on the horizon. Another part of her to learn, another part to love.

Birds begin to chatter. The sky lightens, washed grey. We stand back from the canvas and observe our work.

The end of art making is always a choice, a brave one, I think, because the decision to stop is always in tension with the temptation to keep going.

Before us, stairs descend between white clay houses. The edges of these homes are smooth and round. There are small tufts of green wedged between the buildings with pink flowers flecked among the foliage. At the bottom of the stairs, a small platform overhangs the water. The sea is a deep and magnificent blue. In the distance, tired mountains rest on the horizon. The sky is creamy butter melting in the late sun. We've never been to Greece, but we've seen photos, and this is how we picture it.

Above the mountains, at the edge of the sky, we write,

play with me, these Uranian Games, for as long as we shall live

It's done, I say to Caragh. She kisses me on the cheek, says, it is. She flicks off the stage light.

We only manage a few hours of sleep before Marg comes into our room to wake us. She's already dressed, wearing cream pinstripe trousers and a sky-blue blouse. The shirt is cut with a deep neck and structured with wide shoulder pads. Her lips are glossy red with lipstick, her cheekbones shiny with metallic bronzer. Caragh says, you look incredible. Marg grins, I scrub up okay, don't I? Better than okay! I say and she laughs, grabbing our hands, dragging us out of bed. Come on, she says, I need you to help me bring Geoff up.

Even though we've witnessed Geoff withering away, becoming smaller and smaller before our eyes, there is something profoundly disturbing about holding his body in our arms, feeling the ridges of his spine like sharp metal studs. Lifting him, we experience an absence of weight, and I understand the startling truth that so much of him is gone already. His quiet calm, however, is still here, as it has always been. He says softly, I am just so excited.

We dress Geoff in the suit Daphne has sewn for him. It is cream silk with shoulder pads that make him look like he still has shoulders. Caragh combs his hair and trims his moustache, while Marg dusts powder over his nose and cheeks. I tell him, you look so beautiful.

Marg and Geoff sit on our balcony drinking champagne while Caragh and I get ready. Caragh is wearing a knee-length dress that hangs off the shoulders. The pattern is organic shapes in block colours – red, orange, blue and yellow. She wears gold eye shadow and pink lipstick. I put on navy trousers, a thin white blouse and crocodile skin boots. We sing out, we're ready!

Dave and Tony come into the room and Marg pours us each a glass of champagne. When we clink glasses, we all have tears in our eyes.

There isn't enough room for chairs in the courtyard, so everyone stands at the sides, making an aisle with their bodies. Marg wheels Geoff down the aisle in his wheelchair. His face is shiny and soft, his walls having been washed away by the sheer force of this love and he is here, joyous, wide open and alive. Caragh leans against me, nestling her head into my neck. I wrap my arm around her waist, pulling her closer. Marg positions Geoff in front of our painting. He is looking up at it, eyeing our work when Johnny steps out the back door. Ahem! Over here, Geoff! Johnny sings from the top of the aisle, and everyone laughs. Daphne walks Johnny down the aisle. While they move between us, I have my eyes on Geoff. He is beaming, and I believe, for a moment, that he might explode through his paper skin, like he can't possibly contain this much joy. The feeling I have in me is as beautiful as it is heart-wrenching. I learn, in this moment, how the body is kaleidoscopic.

Johnny's suit is sewn from the same cream silk as Geoff's. When he gets to the front of the aisle, he jokes, Honey, you stole my outfit! Geoff laughs. Babe, I wore it first!

Daphne leads the ceremony. All of you, she says, are gathered here as witnesses. You are here to witness the union of two souls who have collided here, in this life, in the most spectacular way. Johnny and Geoff are our friends, our family, our *skin*, and I want you to open your hearts and be present. Because witnessing this love has been, for me at least, one of the greatest honours of my life. I feel privileged to be here, guiding this ceremony for these two lovers who have taught us all so much. And I want to thank you both, for how you've taught me personally that love, in its purest form, is expansion. It is growth. It is partnership, support and bearing witness to each other. Now we have the immense honour of bearing witness to you both today.

Johnny cries during his vows. He says, you have taught me to love without shame, to be myself, wholly and unapologetically, because you have accepted me in all my mistakes and failings. You have taught me that failing is part of the process of making art, and that life is our greatest work. When I arrive at the end of this making, I know that I will be holding the most beautiful artwork, because of you. And for that, I cannot thank you enough.

Geoff's voice is quiet and croaky. We lean in. He says, meeting you was the beginning of my living, because you taught me to shed my inhibitions and live fully, to crowd every hour with friends, loud singing, theatrics, silliness and lovemaking. You have showed me that there is joy everywhere, and I will pass happily, knowing that I have loved and been loved by you for eighteen years, three months and nine days. What a huge privilege this has been. I feel like the luckiest man in the world.

With all the power in me, Daphne says, I pronounce you husband and husband! Johnny bends down and cradles Geoff's shallow cheeks between his hands, leaning in, slowly, to kiss the love of his life.

The table is laden with a Greek feast fit for kings. We eat and drink and then clear the plates aside because the music is on. Geoff is sitting in front of our painting in his wheelchair, watching the backyard transform into a dance floor. Caragh grabs me by the hand and twirls me beneath strings of twinkling fairy lights. And while we are laughing and singing and swaying, moving like wide undulations of ocean, Geoff slips out, quietly, through the door of his body . . . wandering off into the sky, open and free.

limb two

THE OCEAN IS calm as a lake, grey and sleek like metal. The air is still with not the faintest sea breeze. I am helping Gwen take out the rubbish when she gasps. I turn around and see, painted in red across the side wall of the cottage, the word *FAGGOT!*

I look to Gwen. Her eyes are filling with tears. She wipes them away with her sleeve, then says, I've got sugar soap inside, let me get a bucket.

We fill a bucket with hot water and sugar soap, then grab two kitchen sponges. In the cool and quiet grey, we begin to scrub. The paint has already dried and is difficult to wash off, but with enough repetition, the letters begin to fade. We scrub and scrub until Gwen breaks the silence. You must think I'm mad . . .

I don't know what she means by this, so I say nothing.

She takes a deep breath. Exhales. Then she says, staying with him . . . you probably think I'm mad because I didn't leave. But . . . I mean . . . I've always known . . . deep down, I have . . . And . . . well, he's my best friend.

I'm silent for a moment as *her* face flashes behind my eyes. The memory resurfacing, up out of the waters of my deep past, breaching the air of the present. I feel my heart racing, the words *I'll never want you like that* echoing through my body, ringing in my ears, piercing as a siren, even after all these years. I cringe. Then I blurt out, you can't tell Thomas.

Gwen shrinks, ever so slightly.

And because I feel overcome with my own disgust, I say, he wouldn't understand.

Slowly, she takes a breath, mouth quivering. Then, after a long pause, she closes her eyes and nods, says in a hushed voice, you're right . . .

I nod. Swallow and feel the memory pushed back under. Sunk down. As her face resettles on the ocean floor of my body, I feel the strangle of disgust loosen.

Breathe out.

A twisted sigh.

Heart slowing.

Relief.

We have New Year's Eve at the cottage with Hari, Owain and Bryn. At midnight, they carry Morgan out into the garden, where Hari has set up fireworks. We watch them shoot across a silky black sky, bursting in bright sprays of orange, gold and pink, dispersing like seeds blown off a dandelion.

Thomas wraps his arms around me from behind, resting his chin on my shoulder as they all begin singing in Welsh, him whispering the melody into my ear. I hold on to his arms and look around the garden, at everyone's faces lit up by each blast, at their wrinkled joy, at Owain's hand on Morgan's shoulder, at Hari and Bryn full throat singing with their arms around Gwen, and for a brief moment, feel that life is both beautiful and *exploding*.

Thomas and I wake to a milky sky and decide to surprise everyone with breakfast in the garden. We cook bubble and squeak with the leftover roast vegetables from last night's meal, frying them in a pan. Then we make scrambled eggs. Thomas shows me how his nain would make them, with fresh milk and butter in the mixture so that they're extra creamy. Bryn, Hari and Owain, who are all sleeping in the living room, slowly stir, woken by the crackle and pop of our cooking.

That smells delicious, says Hari as he sits up and rubs his eyes.

We thought we might eat in the garden, since the sun's coming out, says Thomas. Surprise Mam and Tad.

Tidy, says Owain.

The men get changed and help us set up the garden table. Even though the sun is out, the winter air is arctic, so we rug up and bring out woollen blankets for extra warmth. The table is almost ready, set with plates, cutlery, a vase of flowers and glasses of orange juice, when Gwen comes out of her room, in her robe and slippers, puffy eyed and hollowed out like a seashell.

Oh, Gwen . . . says Bryn.

She nods, then says very quietly, I lay with him all night . . . He was never alone . . .

I watch Thomas move across the room, like a panicked little kid. He holds back the tears until he's in his mother's arms and burying his face into her shoulder.

Gwen hangs on tight to her son, running her hands through his hair, consoling him. She sobs, I was right there with him.

And I feel myself take half a step back, suffering the weight of this moment like a blow to my chest, becoming winded and breathless. Because Morgan is gone. And I look at this picture, of Thomas wailing in his mother's hold, grieving the father he's always known. And wonder, how will I keep this picture intact? Vowing, *I must.*

limb one

WE LEARN OUR pain.

We bury a friend – Tony.

In fading light, I leave everyone in the living room and find Dave in his room, sitting on the floor, back against the wall. He moved back into Uranian House just a few days ago, and his room is depressingly sparse, yet to be decorated. He's still in his suit from the funeral, his thinning hair combed to one side. I turn on the bedside lamp and pull out two bottles of Coke from behind my back, cracking the tops off and offering him one. He takes the Coke and says, thanks, Little Dave. Then he taps the space on the floor beside him. I sit down and nestle against him. His body, softer than it used to be.

You know, Dave says, when Andrew died all those years ago, my mother rang me to say he'd died in a car accident. She said, you remember Andrew, don't you? Margaret and Peter's son? They lived across the fence ... And I had to pretend like my heart wasn't being ripped out of my chest. I had to just swallow it all and say, yeah, I remember Andrew. How sad for Margaret and Peter ... that's awful. And I remember she said, yes. Just awful ... And then ... she just changed the subject, and she asked me, are you still coming for dinner with the kids this Sunday? And I felt so breathless, but I had to answer, yes, yes, we are, as if I wasn't dying inside. And then she said, I'm cooking a roast chicken. And I had to pretend as if I was excited, as if I could stomach it ... Dave looks at me now through bloodshot eyes, raises his bottle of Coke and says, I'm glad this time I don't have to pretend.

We learn our pain.

We bury a friend – Robin.

We bury a friend – James.

We bury a friend – Brad.

We bury a friend – Teddy.

We bury a friend – Billy.

We bury a friend – Clive.

We bury a friend – Michael.

We bury a friend – Angus.

We bury a friend – Tim.

We bury a friend – Paul.

We bury a friend – Maxwell.

We bury a friend – Richard.

We bury a friend – Ray.

We bury a friend – Daphne.

Daphne is buried in a cream coffin adorned with a wreath hand-made with foliage from a laurel tree.

We have all pooled our money together to buy this coffin and this burial plot, on the hill at Waverley overlooking open ocean, beside Sam. The water is a magnificent whale blue, clipped white by gusts of a screaming southerly. I imagine that this wind has travelled from the end of the earth where glacier-green ice, at the moment of her death, spectacularly cracked, broke off and became part of the sea. I imagine the voluptuous surrender of ice to ocean – an entire continent sacrificing its edge for our Daphne.

Marg tells us the story of the first time she met Daphne, how she'd been kicked out of home by the bastards who'd adopted her, and how Daphne had found her sleeping rough and brought her to Uranian House, where she met Ruby. Marg describes to us how Daphne helped her to shed her shame and love who she was, by loving her ceaselessly. Marg says, Daphne not only introduced me to the love of my life, but she helped me believe I deserved that love. And when Ruby died . . . well, I'm just not sure I'd still be here if it weren't for you, sis. Because you taught me that I'm my strongest when I've got all youse around me. Marg opens her arms and we all huddle in, limbs entangled. All of us, together, weeping for our matriarch.

I don't drink the wine we've bought for Daphne's wake. Something about numbing the enormity of this pain feels like a disservice to her. Because Daphne was the mother of this house, the hard backbone and the soft, tender front. The woman who transformed in order to survive herself. The woman who made it possible for so many of us to survive. The woman who saved me from myself.

When I go upstairs, I find Caragh in bed drawing with oil sticks. As I approach, she holds up the sketch – a laurel tree in full bloom – and asks me, do you want to write something underneath the tree? I nod, silently, and write beneath the roots, *our love bears witness*.

Four decades from now, a disease will sweep across the world, and they will call it a global pandemic, and governments will act and mobilise, and borders will close. The world will be locked down and people will speak of this strange and unprecedented time. Again and again, they will say, this strange and *unprecedented* time. And for those of us who are still alive, we will say, this is not *my* first pandemic.

limb two

THE WINTER IS a cold I've never felt before, relentless and unending. We rarely leave the cottage, except for walks to the top of the headland. Mostly I am reading by the fire or helping Gwen prepare meals. Darkness lingers in the mornings until half nine and arrives prematurely at three in the afternoon. The sun passes low through the sky, meaning the light never reaches the fullness of what's possible. It makes the days feel like they're only partial happenings. We sleep, too, more than we would ordinarily. Partly, I think this is the grief. Partly, it's the way darkness encroaches from the corners. I find myself aching for brightness, even more than I ache for warmth.

Thomas and I are walking along the beach, skimming pebbles across the ocean's skin, when a man turns up at the cottage with Morgan's ashes. Later, Gwen will tell us how he knocks on the door and says rather bluntly, hi, these are Morgan Bateman's ashes. How he hands Gwen the plastic bag, and says, have a good day. How she watches him walk back down the path, out the gate, and get in his car, before she takes another breath.

When we get back to the cottage, Gwen is on the couch, nose pink and eyes teary. Beside her, on Morgan's armchair, sits a small white box with the funeral home's logo embossed on its lid in gold. She says, I didn't know where to put him . . . I had him sitting on the kitchen bench with me, but he never liked cooking. So I put him on the bed in our room, but it was cold in the bedroom . . . So I thought, I'll put him 'ere, in front of the fire, where it's nice and warm.

We drive with Gwen into the mountains. I am sitting in the back seat when my mouth begins to water and I feel my throat constrict. Could you pull over? I manage. I'm gonna be sick.

Gwen slams on the brakes and I throw open my door, hurling this morning's breakfast onto the bitumen. Thomas gets out of his seat in the front and finds a bottle of water for me. I slosh it around my mouth, then spit it on the ground. Gwen suggests I sit in the front. She says, I get sick, too, if I'm sitting in the back for too long, especially on these winding roads.

I swap with Thomas and we set off again, climbing higher and higher into the mountains until we're driving through cloud. I don't vomit again, but the nausea lingers, and it's not until we're parked and on the walking track, with fresh air biting the walls of my lungs, that this morning's sickness feels as if it's loosening its grip on my throat.

Thomas puts his arm around me, feeling better?

I say, yeah, I am.

Good, he says and kisses me on the cheek.

We follow Gwen along a dirt track through grey grass and ragged rock. There are patches of ice, sparkling as they thaw, and the first wildflowers of spring unfurling in the sunshine, petals creamy as buttermilk.

The path twists and forks, and Gwen walks on, knowing this mountain in her bones. We move in silence, ascending, until the path opens out onto the shoulder of this great body of earth. The view is spectacularly vast, the sky soft pink and stretching all around. In the very distance, the ocean is bleeding purple.

He brought me here, says Gwen, when we first started dating. We would walk this path every weekend . . . we were so young . . . standing right here, we were, when your tad asked me to marry him. He looked out there and said, in this whole wide world, you are my best friend . . .

I feel a shiver creep through my body, but I don't say anything. Not now.

Thomas unzips his backpack and pulls out the box of ashes. He passes it gently to Gwen, then puts his arm around her as she kisses the box and hugs it tightly. She takes a big breath, then says, in this whole wide world, you will always be my best friend.

Gwen opens the box and slowly pours the ashes into the wind. Together, we watch a whole life picked up by a stream of air, carried out into a sea of sky.

Over rarebit for breakfast, Gwen says, I'm going to sell this place . . . Too many people I love have passed 'ere. And when you twos leave, well, I don't think I want to be here with all my ghosts.

I contemplate this for a moment, thinking about people as echoes, and how the memory of a person rings louder in rooms they've slept and loved in. I ask her, will you come back with us to Sydney?

Gwen takes a sip of her tea, and says, yes, I think I'd like that.

The week before we're due to fly back to Australia, Thomas rolls over in bed and says, I don't know if I want to be a writer anymore.

I tell him it's the grief talking, that his appetite for words will come back.

But he shakes his head, and says, I'm not so sure it will.

The dying of his dream before it is realised pinches at my heart. I spend two days thinking of how I can revive it. Then I find Gwen in the garden, tending to her roses, and tell her, I have an idea. And I need your help.

We leave the cottage two days before our flight is set to depart, packing our things into the Mini and telling Thomas we're going to spend the time in Cardiff. I say, I've always wanted to see the city's castle.

He scrunches his face as if to ask, *why?*

I say, it's history . . . plus, I want to go to a bookshop. I need a new book for the plane.

This he believes. He says, okay, sure. I know a beautiful store in the city centre. Do you want to sit in the front?

I say, yes, good idea.

We pull out of the drive and begin the journey south under an ashen sky. All along the road's edges are wildflowers, purple, yellow and white. Thomas is quiet in the back seat. I look over my shoulder and see him slumped against the window. I whisper to Gwen, he's asleep.

She grins, whispering, he won't suspect a thing!

As we travel, Gwen tells me the names of the villages we pass through, sharing the old stories of the people who live in them and what each village is famous for.

I gaze out the window as the towering mountains of the north give way to the sloping green hills of the south. The landscape here is less dramatic. It is more forgiving, more supple, smooth arcs slipping into still and quiet coves. The beaches, too, are softer, pale and sandy, unlike the stony shores of the beaches where we've come from.

Gwen pulls up in a village she tells me is named Laugharne. Thomas wakes with the sound of the car doors opening. He rubs his eyes and looks out the window, confused and searching.

Where are we? he asks as he gets out of the car.

Before us, there is a boathouse, white walls with a plum tiled roof and windowsills painted to match. The boathouse is set in a cliff, overlooking the Tâf Estuary. The shallow water shimmers like flakes of gold leaf. Do you know whose house this is? I ask. Thomas shakes his head.

Gwen says, he had a name just like yours, he did.

Thomas's face lights up now in the fresh sunshine. He grins, and says, Dylan Thomas.

I take hold of his hand, leading him down the gravel path towards the boatshed.

We pay for our tickets and enter the home where Thomas lived with his family during the last four years of his life, which is now a museum. I think again of people as echoes, of the memory of Dylan Thomas reverberating through these walls, ringing loudest at his desk, where he wrote the words that a younger Thomas would read, over two decades later, on the other side of the world, to a girl he already wanted to marry. I look across at Thomas, standing by Dylan Thomas's desk, and it's as if I can see those echoes resounding through him. He is all pricked skin and raised hairs, electrified and excited.

We wander through the boatshed and I think of the first summer after we'd met, when I went back to Newcastle for the holidays and read *Under Milk Wood* and felt myself pining for Thomas in a way that made me feel entirely grown up and fully realised.

Thomas says, are you okay?

I suddenly feel my mouth watering and my throat becoming tight again. I shake my head and he hurries me outside, where I throw up into a bush.

Gwen fetches a water bottle from the car. She unscrews the lid and offers it to me, contemplating out loud, funny that you were okay in the car . . .

I spit water onto the ground, wipe my mouth, and tell her, I felt fine in the car, it just came on all of a sudden.

Was it something you ate? Thomas asks.

Only the same food we've had, says Gwen. Then she gasps. You're not pregnant, are you?

I take a moment to respond, trying to think of when I last had a period. It suddenly occurs to me that I haven't bled since before Morgan died. I touch my hand to my belly, and Gwen bursts into tears, pulling me into a tight embrace, sobbing into my neck, I'm gonna be a nain . . . Oh holy heavens, I'm gonna be a nain.

I feel Thomas wrap his arms around us both, kissing my wet face. He buries his head into my shoulder, wordlessly, he laughs with joy.

Before we leave for Cardiff, we walk in dying light through the village churchyard to where Dylan Thomas is buried. Thomas, standing before the simple white cross that marks the poet's final resting place, recites the poem 'Do Not Go Gentle Into That Good Night' from memory, his words ringing through the trees, fanning out across the water in wide ripples, so that the near and far feel not so far apart.

limb one

THERE IS SO much remembering. All the time. Because we are living in the past. Remembering the summers languid and the parties heaving, wishing, always, to return to that beautiful *before*, the one in which we swam and fucked without fear, the one in which everyone was living and alive. At funerals and around dinner tables, we relentlessly remember our dead. Words like *brave* and *kind* and *fabulous* and *smiling* are uttered repeatedly in all our remembering. And there is a great tension in my body, because while I don't want to forget, I also want, selfishly perhaps, to live *now*. To make new memories.

limb two

WE HELP GWEN move back into the apartment she lived in with Morgan in Rozelle. With the money she receives after selling the cottage in Wales, we're able to put a deposit down on a worker's cottage just down the road from her on a quiet, leafy street. We see her often for lunches on her balcony, and every Saturday she and I go to the markets together, filling our bags with fresh fruit and vegetables. And when my parents come down from Newcastle for Sunday roasts at Gwen's, both Mum and Gwen fuss incessantly over my swelling belly. I find it infuriating.

They're just excited, Thomas reminds me.

Our cottage has a fireplace built into the living room wall, a simple kitchen, a bathroom tiled with baby green squares, and two bedrooms. This colour is perfect, I tell Thomas, as we paint the second bedroom eggshell blue.

In the corner of the room, we put together the cot my parents have given us. I make the small bed with fresh, tiny sheets, and lay down a woollen blanket Giulia's mamma has hand-knitted as a gift from their family. Beneath the window that looks onto the courtyard, Thomas sets up his writing desk. He arranges his notebooks, puts his pens in a glass jar. In the centre of the desk, he places his new typewriter and fills it with sheets of paper. When he's finished, he kneels before my growing belly, lifting my shirt and placing his cool palms on my skin. He vows, I'm going to finish my novel before you come world side, my little love. . . I'm going to make you and your mam so proud.

Han asks, when is the housewarming?

We are eating dinner together in the Haymarket, our lips glistening with gelatinous sauce. I wipe my mouth on a napkin and say, oh, I'd not really thought about that yet.

Giulia laughs. What good is getting a house bought for you if not to have a party?

I feel myself digging my heels in as I remind her that we only got the house because Thomas lost a parent. If it were up to him, I say, I'm sure he'd prefer to have his dad.

Han is quick to respond. Not everyone gets a house when their parents die, you know. Some people lose their dad and *still* don't have anywhere to live.

I know *that*, I tell them both adamantly, my skin stinging hot.

A waiter approaches and asks, how is everything?

Han answers, delicious. It's all very delicious.

Great, he says.

I suddenly feel awkward at my defensiveness. My face is flushed, but I swallow my pride and thank the waiter.

Pleasure, he says, before leaving our table to tend to another one.

When he leaves, I apologise to my friends for my reaction. I know you're right, I say. I guess I'm still feeling quite tender . . . but I am grateful too.

Han takes my hand and sighs. We know . . . and it's alright. I get it. You can be fortunate in one way, and still in pain . . . But we are here for you, aren't we, Giulia?

Giulia nods, smiling kindly. Then she claps her hands together and says, should we make it next Saturday, then?

I say, yeah, sure, I'll let Thomas know. I'm sure he'll be excited . . . He's started writing again.

That's great, says Han, I'm glad to hear it.

I suggest we make the housewarming a dinner with readings.

Giulia grins, looks to Han and says, you should read! I love the story you shared with me the other day. She turns to me and says, you'll love it too. It's deeply haunting . . . uncanny in that way that makes you feel all uneasy and anxious.

Ooh, I say, I'm intrigued! I'd love to hear it. Will you share it? Please?

Han says, yeah, sure. I'd love to.

Great! says Giulia, it's a date! I'll let everyone know.

I arrive home from a community birthing class, put my keys down in the bowl and collapse onto the couch. Thomas comes out of the second bedroom, wearing loose denim jeans and a white singlet, barefoot, pen behind his ear. I look at the grin pinching his face and ask, did you have another breakthrough?

He's all giddy and excited, but he shakes his head.

What is it then?

Do you remember before we left for Wales how I made you

send your CV and that essay about H.D. out to the publishing
house that published Han's friend, Maria?

I nod, feeling my heart quicken.

Well, I hate to say I told you so, but one of the publishers
there, Pearl, rang just now while you were out.

And . . . I say, a smile spreading across my face.

She wants to meet with you. She said she read your essay, and
she thinks you have an instinct for story.

She said that?

He laughs. Yes! Those words exactly. And then she said she
believes you'll make a great editor . . . But I could have told you
that already.

I go to jump up, but forget the weight of my pregnant belly,
and clumsily fall back into the couch. Thomas comes over and
helps me to my feet, then embraces me, kissing all over my face.
I throw my head back and laugh at the ceiling, feeling euphoric.
I become heady with exploding stars.

Life, for this time, is swollen with promise and brimming with
possibility. I feel as if everywhere I look, there are new doors to
walk through, and I have the keys. I feel like I'm on the right path,
I say to Thomas. You know, everything feels like it's flowing, or
something. Like it's meant to be.

He grins and says, you're on a roll!

The streets in the CBD are dimmed and cold, even though it's
midday and the sky is bursting blue. I walk through the shadows
of skyscrapers, through gusts of wind that funnel between the
buildings, breathe in and feel full of world, rich with confidence,
shiny and bright.

I meet Pearl in the foyer of a building with grey glass that stretches so high I have to crane my head backwards to see the top. She leads me through the foyer to the lifts where we ride up to level 7. Stepping out, I follow her into the publishing house's communal kitchen. Coffee? she asks. Tea? What can I get for you?

Do you have herbal?

She opens a cupboard and reveals boxes of tea bags and jars of looseleaf. Take your pick, she says.

I'll have peppermint, please.

Pearl gets me a mug and flicks on the kettle. While it boils, she tells me they've only been in this building a few years. Beautiful, isn't it?

I look over my shoulder through the wide glass windows and take in the view of the harbour. I say, yes. I wouldn't mind looking out there all day.

She laughs, it can be distracting. I sometimes find myself looking at all the tiny little boats, imagining where they're coming from, or where they're headed. Have you ever been sailing?

I shake my head.

We had our Christmas party on a yacht last year. It sounded like a good idea, but with the boat rocking, and all of us as drunk as we were, it was not so romantic in practice.

I smile and say, no, I guess not.

The kettle boils and Pearl makes my tea, then says, let's go into my office.

She closes the glass door, sits down behind her desk and motions for me to sit opposite. Then she says, I loved your essay. I'd never considered H.D.'s poetry through that lens before. Your politicised reading of botany in her work was especially engaging. I mean, I was already familiar with *Sea Garden*, but you showed me the work from a new angle. You drew from it something I hadn't seen. That's why I wanted to meet with you.

Thomas is waiting for me when I get home. So, he says, before I put my bag down, how did it go?

She's offered me a one-month internship! And it's *paid*! She knows I'm pregnant . . . I point at my belly and say, well, I mean, *obviously*. But she said that if I do well during the internship, there might be a job for me next year when I want to go back to work . . .

Thomas jumps up and down, squealing and laughing.

I'll be reading manuscripts, I say, and giving notes. I guess I'm kind of her assistant?

When do you start?

Next week!

We invite Gwen to our housewarming. She arrives carrying a bowl of trifle and a bottle of wine. Giulia and I are laying plates and cutlery around a table we've borrowed from her family and set up in our living room. Doesn't this look nice, says Gwen as she eyes the tealight candles and vases of native wattle we've arranged down the middle of the table.

Our friends begin to arrive and Thomas proudly introduces his mam to each of them. He's equally delighted when he tells our friends about my internship.

That's great! says Han, smiling. I just got an internship too! And the building is just down the road from yours! Maybe we can have lunches together?

I'd love that, I say, embracing her. Congratulations!

Giulia grins. It's all happening for you!

215

limb one

CARAGH CUTS MY hair off. I am shaking and mistake the feeling for fear, because I watch the hair land in fat chunks on our bedroom floor and expect to be overcome by loss. Then she says, done, and turns me towards the mirror. I realise that the nerves were the beginning of excitement, expansion, evolution. I look at my face, at my jawline and cheekbones, now pronounced and sharper. I think of myself as a kid, back when I was lean muscle and all limb. Before my body swelled and became something like a shadow, outside and beyond, stalking the edge of me. Now I look in the mirror and there's no shadow. Only myself, in full, bright light. Because I didn't necessarily feel wrong, until suddenly it now all feels right.

Oh no! Caragh says, worried at my explosion of tears. Do you hate it? I laugh, through this mess of snot, shaking my head. I could not love it more! She breathes a sigh of relief and says, good. And then she kisses my mouth. You look very handsome, Claude. I grin so hard my cheeks hurt. Pinched by a feeling of euphoria that is as fresh as it is electric. Handsome, I say, rolling the word around in my mouth. I do, don't I?

There is an entire team at Bart's Gallery to hang our art. Berenice, who goes by Bunny, is curating our show. She has cold hands and sharp teeth. Her silver hair is cut hard across her cheek. She pours us each a champagne while we watch as our works are measured and installed. I think of our early shows in friends' living rooms and garages, of how drunk we'd get every time we exhibited, of the arguments we had while hanging our work ourselves in warehouses and studios and artist collectives. And now, here we are, exhibiting at Bart's Gallery, bubbles in hand, looking at each other in disbelief. Caragh whispers in my ear, we've *made* it. We are giggling hot breath. Then Caragh squeezes my hand, and Bunny, with the cold hands and sharp teeth, says, I wouldn't do that, not *here*.

At the entrance of the gallery, large block letters are printed on the glass: *Uranian Games*. Beneath them, Caragh has drawn, in white paint pen, the outline of a placard. It reads in small handwritten letters: *trespassers will be prosecuted!*

We are standing on the kerb rolling cigarettes. Caragh's hands are shaking. It's okay, I tell her. But she shakes her head, eyes watery. I want to go back, she whispers. And I know exactly what she means, because in this moment, we are met by the brutal realisation that our access to this space, *HERE*, comes at a cost. *Here* is hostile and hinged on our silence. *Here*, they are happy to sell what we have made, so long as we don't tell anyone where we made it . . . where it's *from*.

Because back there, before the artist collectives and the studios and the warehouses, before the bar, before the garages and the living rooms, we are in bed, between the sheets, fucking.

I throw my cigarette on the concrete, stub it out with my boot and put my mask on. It is shiny silver. Caragh's is metallic purple. The patrons are all arriving now, putting on the masks we've placed at the front of the gallery. Men in steamed suits and iron-pressed shirts, with shiny leather shoes. Women in silk dresses that flow across the polished floors of Bart's Gallery.

Inside, we are introduced to patrons as artistic collaborators. Then, while Caragh is talking about the placard drawn over the glass at the entrance, Bunny pulls me away to speak to someone else. This man points to a work and asks me about the sentence at the centre, and I want to tell him that I conceived the words *in this great migration south, you pull my limbs apart* with her hand inside me. But I can't, can I? They came to me in a dream, I say. He takes a sip of his wine. The Surrealists, he says, were fascinated by dreams. André Breton, Paul Éluard, Robert Desnos . . . I nod my head, politely, then say, Claude Cahun. Oh, this man says, I've not heard of him . . .

I am introduced to another man. He compliments our work, telling me how he finds the interplay of text and imagery very interesting. I've seen this done so haphazardly, he says, but this collaboration is remarkably seamless. The two are so enmeshed . . . I want to ask him, don't you understand? *I love her!*

Caragh and I find each other at the back of the gallery beside the drinks table. When no one is looking, I crack open the door to the storage closet. Come on, I say. She grins and follows me in. We close the door behind us. The air is starved dark and dust, but when she lifts my mask and kisses my mouth, I don't care that we are hiding, because the sweetness of this secret is sacred. It is ours, and ours only.

There is a commotion at the entrance. I excuse myself from yet another collector telling me about our art and make my way to the front of the gallery. Bunny is there with her security, blocking the doorway. I can hear Johnny's voice. Fuck you, then! he shouts as Bunny closes the door. Through the glass, I see Johnny and Dave strut back across the road, hand in hand. They are both in dresses and big hair. There are murmurs passed seedily through the gallery. Fuck this, I mutter under my breath, suddenly wanting to rip all the works off the walls. I want to scream. *You do not deserve this!*

I grab Caragh's hand and ask, who is this even for? She says, come on, let's just go.

The night sky is clear and the air is crisp. Caragh is shivering a little, so I wrap my arm around her shoulders. Ahead of us, four men stumble out of the back door of a pub. And because I am sick of walking beside and not *with* her, I don't take my arm off her shoulders. Even as we near them, even as one of them mutters *dykes* as they pass. And because I am sick of everything I hold sacred being desecrated and defiled, I turn and spit on him. He is open-mouth shocked, for a moment, wiping my spit off his cheek with his fist. Then he swings at me. He misses my face and clips my shoulder. I trip backwards, landing on the concrete. I feel something pop in my wrist. The man grins, spits down on my body and snarls, you're dead.

limb two

WE BOOK A table at a fancy restaurant in the city after my final day working for Pearl. Thomas says, it's important to celebrate every victory. Over a plate of duck confit with caramelised vegetables, and another plate of buttery spaghetti strewn with pipis, I say to Thomas, I actually have something to tell you.

Yeah?

I know you didn't want me to . . .

He frowns. Yes . . .

But I showed Pearl the prologue and first chapter of your book.

His face goes pale, his eyes widened by fear.

Don't panic! I say, laughing. She wants to read more!

Are you serious?

Yes! I reach across the table and take hold of his hand. She loves your writing. Like, *loves* it!

He lets out a heavy breath. Oh my *God*, you scared the shit out of me!

I raise my glass of mineral water to his glass of champagne and say, it's important, remember? To celebrate every victory.

When we're finished, Thomas opens the door for me, lightly touching my back as I step from the burnt butter glow of the restaurant, out onto the street. The night sky is clear and the air is crisp. I take my woollen scarf out of my pocket and twirl it round my neck. I am shivering a little, so he wraps his arm around my shoulder.

That was delicious, I tell him.

It was, says Thomas, wasn't it?

Especially the duck.

Yes, especially the duck! My belly is brimming.

I love how you describe things, I say, as I slip my hand beneath my jumper and smooth the front of my dress over my round belly. She's been quiet tonight, I say, I've barely felt her move.

He laughs. What are you going to do if we have a boy?

We won't, I say. I just know it.

How can you be so sure?

Because she talks to me, in my dreams. I've held her already.

I cannot wait to hold her, Thomas says and kisses my cheek. And for you to be a mother.

Up ahead, a crowd is gathered on the sidewalk at the mouth of an art gallery. People are holding glasses of red wine or flutes of champagne. Some are smoking as they talk. They're all beautifully dressed and wearing masks. One man in a cream suit is wearing a mime's mask, white, like teeth. Another woman is wearing a Venetian mask with gold shading around the eyes and an elongated nose, thin as an ibis beak. Thomas asks, how are you feeling, my love? Should we go in?

I feel fine, I say, but we don't have masks.

Thomas points to a couple nearby. Look, he whispers, they don't have them either. I'm sure it won't matter.

Okay, I say, grinning. Let's check it out.

Thomas takes hold of my hand and we weave through the crowd. Someone is smoking a clove cigarette, making the air taste sweet. I see the illustration of a placard drawn on the front window of the gallery with paint. Thomas whispers in my ear, trespassers will be prosecuted!

Then he squeezes my waist at the very point he knows I'm most ticklish. The touch makes me jump. I am giggling as I playfully swat his hand away. He takes my hand again and leads me into the gallery.

The works adorning the walls inside are unlike anything I've ever seen. Each canvas is a blend of photo collage and paint. Glossy images of masks and genitalia, teeth and unfurling flowers, eyes and open mouths, are cut and pasted on the canvases and enmeshed in and around painted bodies. Entangled limbs are depicted in thick daubs of oil, with words etched into the paint. I stand before one work in which seven splayed legs open to the words,

we are skin

and suddenly, I feel a wetness between my thighs. I touch my hand to it and go pale at the sight of blood saturating my dress. Thomas, I say. Something's wrong.

223

An ambulance arrives in a blur of red and blue. Thomas's face is glossy with panic. I roll away from the sting of bright light, wincing. It's okay, I hear him say, it's going to be okay.

But I know already not to believe him.

limb one

THERE AREN'T WORDS for this. For this horror that is indescribable. Language, I think, falls short, as Caragh steps forward into his path and his clenched fist meets her face. Language falls short. Because she falls. Slowly, she falls,

f

                a

        l

    l

               i

    n

                    g

through air

spiralling down through all the years lived, back to the very beginning, into the darkness

from which she was birthed
and into which she ends, her skull cracked open on concrete.

The language itself is unimaginable because *this* is unimaginable. Because there is blood trickling out of her nose and out of her ears. I am watching the love of my life leaving her body, pooling around her beautiful head in a red halo.

The vision is of two lives lived together, soft wrinkles around the eyes, dying somewhere in the very distance.

The view is Caragh, dead on the sidewalk.

limb two

Something happens to me now that makes the words *we cannot find a heartbeat* pass through me with freakish clarity. Like I understand, like it all makes sense. She is dead and I must deliver her anyway. It's okay, I whisper to Thomas, I can do this. I will do this.

And so, I close my eyes, silencing the beeping of machines and the voice of the midwife at St Vincent's telling me, *push, now breathe, and again, push,* and slowly begin my descent into the well.

It is all cold shadow and the walls are slippery with moss, but I sing to her, our lullaby so that she knows, don't worry, baby. Here I am, I'm coming for you. With my bare hands and feet, I descend slowly, down into the heart. All I can hear is the quiet dripping of water as thin streams seep through cracks in the brickwork and fall, blue droplets landing softly on black sand at the base of the well. She isn't breathing, but I know this already. Almost there, my love, I whisper, as I descend the last stretch of wall and touch my bare foot to the sand. Volcanic black grains shift beneath my weight, cool at the surface but warmer underneath, the way ash holds the heat of last night's fire. I kneel before her body, still, but not sleeping. I touch my fingertip to her soft cheek and whisper, my little love, I've waited so long to meet you.

In the calm grey, I take off my shirt and scoop up her tiny body and clutch her against my naked chest. I hold her here, for a long time, for hours, for years, a whole life, perhaps, in my arms, breath held. Until, finally, I breathe out and whisper, okay, baby, it's time for us to go.

Gently, I stand with her in my arms, touch my lips to her tiny forehead and kiss her softly in this damp darkness. With my shirt, I tie her tiny body against my torso, slinging her around my belly so that she's tucked in, ready for the climb out. Okay, little love, I whisper, it's time. I reach up, grab hold of the wall and begin the climb, upwards, out of the well, into the light. Slowly, one hand in front of the other, reaching up, up, up. Until I touch the lip of the well and climb out into the world and open my eyes.

I see Thomas. He's beside my bed, one hand on our daughter's small back, the other hand cradling my cheek. I look down at her resting on my chest, and then back to Thomas, at the tears in his eyes, at his face flushed, and think, this picture is *almost* perfect.

Everyone has left the room to give us space. We are still, here, with our still baby, for a long time. Until Thomas whispers, I love you, to our daughter, and I feel the shock beginning to wear off. Adrenaline fades into blood and the container of my grief disintegrates. Suddenly, I am overflowing. And because this pain is sidesplitting, I start to scream. Whole body shaking, I scream until my throat is ripped raw and nurses rush in to sedate me.

When I wake, Thomas is by my side, sobbing. She's dead, I say, isn't she? He nods, yes, my love. She's our angel now.

limb one

I LEARN THAT *Caragh* in Irish means 'beloved'.

The name, *Caragh*, also means 'friend'.

I am not allowed to see my beloved when I arrive at St Vincent's, because I am a friend.

Only family is let into the chilled room where they are asked to identify her body. Only family is given the space and time to say goodbye.

A doctor tells me I have broken my wrist. I look down at my flesh, all bulging and blue. The doctor asks if I have been given any medication for the pain. I shake my head. My bone is split in two and I can barely feel the ache of it. He requests a nurse to fetch me some pain relief. He says, you will need this when the shock wears off.

I can't remember the phone number for Uranian House. And so, I sit here, sieving sand for the right numbers, the nurse growing increasingly frustrated as we wake another angry parent who complains this call has woken their kids. Finally, I get it right, and the nurse asks Marg to please come down to the hospital.

By the time she, Dave and Johnny make it to my bedside, I've been put into a soft cast to hold my broken limb together until the morning when they can take me into surgery. They ask, are you okay? What happened? I open my mouth, but my tongue is a marshland. Nothing I'm saying is making any sense, my words are sloppy and all mushed together. Slow down, slow down, says Dave. Then Marg asks, where's Caragh?

The shock is beginning to wear off. Adrenaline fades into blood and the container of my grief disintegrates. I overflow. And because this pain is sidesplitting, I scream. Whole body shaking, I scream until my throat is ripped raw and nurses rush in to sedate me.

When I wake, Marg, Dave and Johnny are asleep in the chairs beside my bed. Slowly, I climb out, careful not to wake them. I'm in a hospital gown, my arm hugged across my chest in a sling. I creep out of the room and down the hall, searching for the love of my life.

I peer through glass and behind curtains, until I arrive at a window and see Caragh's parents at the foot of a bed. I recognise them from photographs Caragh kept in our room. Her three brothers are there with her parents, all holding each other as they weep. The curtain beside her bed is half drawn. All I can see are her feet. Caragh's mother grips her daughter's ankles as she cries hard against the night.

I think of an argument we had once, when Caragh went home for Christmas. *We* are your family, I'd said. *We're* your skin. Be with us this year, please. I remember how she'd shaken her head and told me, I have two families. How when she left, I cried to Dave, telling him, but Caragh is *my person*. I remember how Dave had assured me, and you are hers . . . How I'd fired back, then why isn't she *here*? How Dave had taken me in his arms and said, Little Dave, you can't just ask her to abandon a huge part of herself. She's as Irish and as Catholic as she is gay. Let her be all of it.

I hear Caragh's dad tell his wife that he's going to make her a tea. He opens the door to Caragh's room, and I step back from the window. He's startled by me standing here in the hallway. Looking at me with a puzzled expression, he asks softly, can I help you? I try to speak, but no words come out. Are you looking for someone? I take another step back, and after what feels like an eternity, I think of something Caragh told me once: *my silence is a gift*. Finally understanding what she meant, I shake my head and whisper, no, I'm sorry . . . wrong room.

limb two

HER DEATH IS like a bird slamming into a window. The sudden shock that the sky has limits. That my motherhood was a trick of light.

limb one

HER DEATH IS like a bird slamming into a window. The sudden shock that the sky has limits. That our liberation was a trick of light.

limb two

WHAT I DON'T imagine is the smallness of the coffin, or how enormous our friends and family will look gathered around it, imposing, like giants. I don't imagine how this will affect me, how it will crush me, to see her coffin overwhelmed by bodies that got to grow fully. The snatching of her life before it became one feels unbelievably cruel. My life, as shiny as it was, opalescent like the insides of an oyster shell, is turned over, and everything becomes scaly and sharp.

Thomas reads from *Deaths and Entrances*. His copy, with its soft red cover, is well-loved, worn and fraying at the edges. When he looks up from the page, his eyes are soaked. He blinks and tears run across his skin in thin streams.

Your heart, Thomas says, is luminous.

We bury our baby at Waverley, in a plot overlooking the sea. As we lower her coffin into the ground, the water puckers and we see a pod of dolphins, gliding inside unbroken waves.

From this height atop the headland, the waves, fanning out as far as the horizon, look like ripples in a blue pond.

I am at once overcome by the way the ocean is both ever-lasting and finite, because as expansive as this water appears, it suddenly dawns on me that all seas have borders.

limb one

In 1933, THE leader of the Surrealist group, André Breton, and the Surrealist poet Paul Éluard created a survey in which they asked readers, *what is the most important meeting of your life? And to what degree did this meeting seem to come by lucky chance? And to what degree did this meeting seem to come by necessity?*

I first saw you in a crowd of people and placards. We were demonstrating. Existing in a space that denied our existence. That actively erased us. And yet, there we were.

I first saw you and you didn't look remarkable. You were wearing a casual black t-shirt and faded black jeans. Your hair was pulled tight. You didn't look particularly striking, and yet, I was entirely struck, the way lightning turns sand to glass.

I found myself drawn to you. Amid the chanting and the cries, I saw that your body was full of opposites. Anguish and confidence.

Betrayal and unity. Horror and joy. You carried yourself like you were crumbling alive.

You would have urged me not to name this meeting the most important meeting of my life, but rather, the most important meeting of my life thus far, arguing that meaning is determined by context, that significance exists in flux . . . but I disagree.

I already know it. You are the most important meeting of my life.

Because you came over me like a wave. And I dove through the belly of the ocean, where I have been, ever since.

With you, I could exist underwater. And in the beginning, I panicked. Because everything we've ever been told tells us we cannot breathe underwater. I wanted to stay, but I thought, I need air, I need air. This isn't how we are supposed to live, they say. But by both luck and necessity, my body changed. My lungs became gills.

I had learnt to exist otherwise, and to live entirely in it.

You are the most important meeting of my life. And I dislike the proposition of the Surrealists, pitting luck and necessity against each other, as if they sit at opposite ends of a line. As if, by degree, I could position this meeting closer to one end than the other.

But our love is full of opposites. We are each other's muse, but we are also each other's collaborator. Our love is hard edges and soft, porous borders. Because we are our own people even as we spill into each other.

And now our love is dead and living. Finite and timeless. Heartbreaking and heartbroken. Because my love for you is so alive it flows into the valley of the dead.

I met you at the end of a series of random occurrences that have lined up one after the other from the beginning of time. I met you as a result of luck and out of necessity.

Over and over, I had thought that I would die young. Until I met you, and you kissed me beneath a car, and I thought, I want to live forever.

That is how you made me feel. You made me feel like even if we were to live to one hundred it would still be unfair, because we would only have eighty years together, and I want even more.

I am tempted to call this desire for life the greatest gift you gave me, but I refuse. Because people who are murdered are not obliged to give gifts to the living.

It is the still living who are charged with the responsibility to keep the dead alive.

And so, I will keep you alive the only way I know how . . . in my body. By luck and necessity, I met you and you painted on the underside of my flesh. Now I will keep you alive by love, loving you ceaselessly. In every movement of every murmuration.

I don't deliver this eulogy, because I don't go to Caragh's funeral.

I never find out whether she is burnt or buried. I never find out where her ashes are scattered or what words are etched into her headstone.

Alone in our bed, I picture her parents and her brothers in the church singing hymns and remind myself that my silence is my final gift.

Dave says, my sweets, there's no such thing as closure.

I burn my eulogy and instantly regret it.

Choked. I am desperately alone in my grief, because Johnny is carrying the loss of Geoff, and Marg is carrying the loss of Daphne and Sam, and Dave is carrying the loss of Tony, and no one has any room to hold anyone else.

I wonder, what is the weight of my grief if it cannot be carried by others? What is the measure?

limb two

THERE ARE BRIEF windows when I forget, and then the truth comes swinging back into the present like a great chunk of concrete, shattering the glass, obliterating me.

When I tell Thomas we need to pack down the nursery, that I want to donate the cot to charity, he says, but we can try again.

I say, I cannot do this again.

And he begs, telling me it's the grief talking, that I'll feel differently with time.

I shake my head and say, you're not listening to me. I will *not* do this again.

And he opens his mouth to protest, but reconsiders when I say, you cannot make me. Okay?

Thomas sighs and walks out of the room. I hear him screaming in the living room and hold my breath until he's finished. He comes back in with a screwdriver and says, okay then. And begins unscrewing the legs of the cot.

Thomas wordlessly gets out of bed every morning, makes a cup of tea, and goes into the other room to write. He stays there all day, only coming out to make a sandwich or to brew another cup of tea. Sometimes, he takes a teapot in with him so he doesn't have to come out as often.

He becomes so quiet with me, barely sharing anything. He's saving his words, I think, for his novel, for his characters and his scenes, for another world.

When he comes out of the room one afternoon and says, I've done it . . . it's done.

And I feign a smile and say, that's great, congratulations.

He scrunches up his face and asks, aren't you happy for me?

I laugh. *Happy?*

I read Thomas's manuscript lying on the grass down by the harbour. Runners run past. Walkers walk past. And all I can feel is a deep resentment for the way the world just gets on, like nothing has happened at all.

When I read the final page, the last sentence, I close the bound pages and look down at the water's surface, pale and perished, and feel myself utterly bewildered.

It occurs to me how strange it is that he has written a happy ending, that the characters are not destroyed by their losses, but made sun drunk with silver linings. The neat bow he ties around the story is limp and lifeless. I don't believe any of it.

When I hand back the manuscript and he looks at me with an excited grin, anticipating my praise, I genuinely despise him.

limb one

You FIND ME, most often, in that small corridor between night and day, when the sky is washed out white and I feel your hand clenched in tight fistfuls of thigh. Feel your breath in my throat and think, oh, here you are. Tell me, where have you been?

and you smile and say, my love, I never left.

For a moment, this is true.

I will laugh, or cry, on
choked joy,
the softest joy . . .
Joy, unbearable.

I will tell you how much I've missed your tongue dragged over my belly. I will tell you how much I've missed you holding my cunt in your mouth. And as you reach your hand inside me, you will say, I've been here, right here, the whole time.

Before, I would try to be quiet. These walls are paper thin . . .

You said once, scream for me. And I didn't. And maybe you felt embarrassed, because you never asked again.

I held back, always, held it all at the back of my throat. Why did I do that? Scared to rejoice? Shame at the thought of others listening? Shame that they'd hear me? Shame at my pleasure? Shame straddling everything I love. Shameful body. Shame! What a shame . . .

Scream for me, you say, tongue wet in my ear. I am fucking myself: Do you hear me now? I arc my spine and let go of my throat and all my pleasure rushes out through open teeth, through the ghost of you, through these paper-thin walls, into another room, out onto the street. Something unruly and animal, I feel all of you. Here, with me, haunted. I scream for all the times I was quiet, for all the times I held back, for all the times I made myself small. I scream and find myself beautiful and exploding.

You make me unbearably wet, still. And I wonder, is it wrong to be turned on by someone who is dead?

I fuck the ghost of you and learn that grief is not sadness. Grief is the body cut open, flows of blood and joy and salt and ache and words and memory and memories never made. Grief is undoing.

Grief is wanting flesh, yearning for a voice. Grief is fear of forgetting . . . a face . . . the contour of a hip . . . your brilliant red hair . . . Grief is wondering what could have been made and what could have become. Grief is what if. Grief is endless cycles of why, and I wish I didn't. Grief is the guilt of the living, of my living. Grief is the sobbing into my birthday cake, because I'm older than you, now. Grief is the building of a world without you in it.

Then there's the less obvious . . . the part no one writes about. How grief is horny. How I bend myself over the bedhead and feel your fingers in my arse. Real and imagined, grief is pining for your touch. Grief is being wet for a ghost.

Grief is not sadness. It is a kaleidoscope of desires. Like white light refracted through skin.

Sadness, I think, is the object.
And grief is the negative space.

limb two

I PEDAL OUT of our driveway with his words ringing in my ears, *what do you mean you don't know where?*

On my bicycle, I race out of our cul-de-sac, along one avenue, then another, flying along Darling Street as dusk bleeds blue into pink. My lungs ache and my calves are ablaze, but I keep pedalling, hoping my breath will drown out the argument playing, on loop, behind my eyes.

You don't get it!

How can I? You won't let me in!

You haven't been *here*.

I have! I've been right here.

No, Thomas. *I* have been *right here . . .* by *myself,* this whole time!

Honey, I haven't left you . . .

You have no idea what I'm going through! The closest you get to me is when you're asleep!

What *we're* going through . . .

Don't touch me!

For fuck's sake. I'm grieving, too, you know! She was my daughter too!

I said don't touch me!

Hey . . . come on, now . . .

You don't know anything, Thomas!

Then talk to me!

You've been off in your own world for years! You missed your mum's birthday . . . And the anniversary of your dad's death! I mean, fucking hell, you didn't even know your dad was gay!

What?

Yeah. That's right! So don't tell me you've been *here*!

What did you just say?

You heard me.

Stop! Where are you going?

I don't know where!

What do you mean *you don't know where*?

Ahhhhhh!!!!!!!!! I scream now as I round a corner. The world passes by in a blur of concrete, brick and white streetlight. I pedal and pedal until I am braking to a halt at a leafy dead end. The park before me is sprawling lawns and wide paths that lead to the water. The last of the day's light drips through the trees, soaking in where it lands. I get off my bike and wheel it over to the kerb. Three women walk out of Dawn Fraser Baths, still in their bathing suits, towels wrapped around their waists and red marks around their eyes from their goggles. They are chatting and laughing as they walk. One woman catches my eye and stops. She looks at me, cocks her head slightly and says, are you okay?

And because I don't know how to hold this tension, I laugh. The sound is unruly and guttural, but the woman doesn't flinch, she just stands there, body soft, her wet, silver hair catching under the streetlights. This woman – a stranger – smiles gently and I burst into tears.

She says to her friends, I'll see you next week . . .

We can stay, another woman says.

No, no, I think we'll be okay. The woman turns to me, and says, won't we?

I nod, sobbing into my hands, utterly mortified.

She waves goodbye to her friends and then says, do you want to sit down? She motions to a bench at the entrance to the park. As we walk over to it, she tells me her name is Dot . . . Well, it's Dorothy Aziza, but only my mum called me that. And she's been gone a long while now.

That's a nice name, I mutter.

Dot reaches into her swimming bag and rifles through it. Finally, she pulls out a pair of trousers, reaches into the back pocket and draws out a handkerchief. My pa used to tell me to always carry a handkerchief in your pocket, Dot says as she passes it to me. He'd say, Dot, you'll never regret it!

I take the handkerchief, wipe my eyes and am about to blow my snotty nose when I look at her and hesitate.

It's okay, she says, that's what it's for!

I half smile and confess, I didn't know if that was bad etiquette . . . I don't know . . . I guess I don't do this often . . .

What? Cry to a funny old lady in a park?

I laugh at this. No, I say, not often.

She laughs now too.

I introduce myself and go to give back the handkerchief.

And when she grins and says, oh, you can keep it, love . . . I remember, with startling clarity, how Thomas had laughed softly, small creases at the edges of his smile, and said, you can keep it. How I'd blushed with embarrassment. How I'd felt so disarmed by him. How I'd thought to myself, that very first day, I want to be around this person, *always*.

I thank Dot and take a deep breath, picturing Thomas now, at home at his desk, silently working away on his third draft, and think, two things can be true at once.

Across the road, more women are filing out of the pool. It's ladies' night, says Dot. Do you swim?

Night is falling around us, and I can see she is starting to shiver. You're cold, I say.

I am, she says. She is smiling but her teeth are chattering.

I'm okay, I say, standing up. I'm going to be okay . . .

Are you sure?

I nod. Yes. Thank you. Thank you very much.

Okay, then, she says as she walks me back over to my bike. You know, swimming is good for the soul . . . especially in good company. We all swim together every week. You should come one time . . . see if you like it.

I climb onto my bike and tell her, thank you, Dot. I'll definitely think about it.

She unlocks her car, opens the door. As she's about to get in, she winks at me and says, let the water carry what you can't.

When I get home, Thomas is in the living room on the couch. I put my bike against the wall in the hallway and stop at the entrance to the living room. He looks up at me with red eyes and asks, how did you know?

Your mum told me.

And you kept it from me? For all this time?

I feel myself shudder as a memory rises in me, of a girl over the fence. Of how being hated was easier than pining. I feel the sharp pang of shame, of guilt, of remorse. The weight of my own dank secrets heavy in me. I remember the feeling of my jaw locked shut. *I'll never want you like that.* How I'd screamed.

Then Thomas shakes his head and says, I'd have loved him anyway.

And I feel sick at the thought of what could have become.

My tad died thinking I would have been ashamed of him. How dare you rob me of the chance to tell him it's okay.

limb one

I WANT TO tell you that I found your killer, that he's going to jail. But I can't, because word on the street is, he's a cop. Because he is protected, and we are not. Because his colleagues make this go away. Because he makes you go away and then it all goes away.

I want to tell you that he's been charged and sentenced. But there isn't this sentence to tell. Instead, you were sentenced to death and now your sentence ends in his ongoing and eternal unravelling sentences of free walking greatness.

limb two

THOMAS AND I avoid each other at home, and I learn how loneliness is felt most acutely in the presence of another person when the intimacy is gone. No touch. No words. Only sleepless nights faced away from each other in bed.

The wait for Tuesday feels long and unending.

I am quivering with nerves as I pay my entry fee for the pool. I've got my bag with my brand-new swimsuit, goggles and blue swimming cap, and a towel slung over my shoulder. The woman at the front counter says, the change rooms are over there, and points to a doorway across the pool.

Inside the change rooms, women are undressing without towels. I am surprised by this, by the casualness with which they unbutton their shirts and drop their skirts, how they don't break their conversations when they pull off their undies.

I wrap my towel around my waist and slowly take off my trousers, feeling awkward as I shimmy into my flash new swimsuit. I wonder if they'll notice that it's never been worn, that I've got all the gear and no idea. I take my arms out of my jumper and pull the swimsuit up over my torso, looping my arms through, so that I'm entirely inside the swimsuit before I take off my jumper and unwrap my towel.

Looking down at my body, at the leftover flesh of my pregnancy, I feel alien to these limbs. For weeks now, I've been avoiding mirrors, painfully reminded always by the weight of my own loss. Because my body remains soft for holding and nursing and swaying. And my breasts remain swollen with offering. And the hormones inside make me feel things that aren't true.

I get my swimming cap out of my bag and look around to see how other women are putting on their caps. I watch them tie their hair back and tie mine into a tight bun at the back of my head. Then I attempt to put the cap on by myself.

Tricky doing that alone, says a woman a few metres down the bench from me. She puts her bag in her locker and then comes over. Let me help you, she says. Here, hold it like this . . .

Thanks, I say, as she pulls the cap over my head in one swift motion.

I'm Rosa.

I tell her my name as I find my goggles at the bottom of my bag.

I've not seen you here before. First time?

I nod. Yeah . . . I swam growing up, but it's been a while.

She smiles and says, better late than never.

At this moment, Dot appears and says, you're here!

I grin, yeah, nice to see you.

You too! And I see you've met my friend Rosa.

Yes, she helped me with my swimming cap.

Tricky things those are . . . Like most things, they're best when you have a friend to help you.

I dive in and am taken by the sudden cold. It makes everything feel light and electric. I begin to swim, but I feel awkward, gangly and uncoordinated. I pause halfway up the pool, treading water in the middle of the lane. I've got tears welling and my throat feels tight with panic. Dot swims up behind me. Don't worry, she says, we all swim at our own pace here . . .

I must look terrible, because she smiles gently and says, how about you try breaststroke for a few laps? It's a bit easier on the body.

I nod. Okay, yeah . . . I'll try that.

Dot swims off and I slowly begin to swim again, moving my arms around, like I'm scooping up water and pulling it into my heart. Dot is right, this does feel easier. My pulse is beginning to settle as I move into flow, pull, breath, kick, pull, breath, kick, pull, breath, kick.

I learn that if pain is noise in the body, the absence of pain is breathtaking silence.

limb one

DEATH DOES SOMETHING to us. It charges us, the *still* living. It makes our blood thin, so thin and watery that everything feels precarious, like I might bleed out through a paper cut.

I find photographs of us one day. They are portraits we took of each other, naked in grey light. In one, you spread your legs before the lens, gently pulling at the edges of yourself, revealing, for me, your interior. I took it in the moments after we'd made love, but before you'd wiped away your cum, and smiled. I hold the picture in my hand, fingers shaking. Because there it is, captured – the soft traces of your ecstasy. Proof that we loved. Proof that you were here. I look to another photo. One of your body blurred. Because you moved as I took it, and now you're in this photo, in motion forever. Then I find a portrait you took of me, eyes in focus, but my lips are fuzzy. I must have been speaking. I stare at this photo for a long time, for it, too, is evidence that I was here, that my body was there, that you were here, listening. But what do I say? What am I saying?

I am in the bar when I overhear Stella say how Caragh died. A king hit. That's what she calls it. I stride over and slam my drink down. The force breaks the glass, and my beer explodes across the table. The glass has cut my finger, and now the table is a mess of frothy blood. Marg comes over from behind the bar, shakes her head and sighs. Fuck, I mutter, I'm sorry, Marg. She has a tea towel slung over her shoulder, which she uses to mop up the mess. Don't say sorry to me, she says. My eyes glass over, blurring the picture of Stella and Kelly who are staring back at me, mouths gaping. You're wrong, I say to Stella, what you said . . . it's wrong. And then I walk out.

In our bed, alone, in the early hours of the morning, I realise, we need a new term. A new word to detract from the glory. To make *hit* mean: gutless, spineless, heartless. To make it clear how much is taken. And how much is now missing. To make it clear that the body is dismembered by this *hit*. That lives are cleaved apart. I remember, suddenly, with startling clarity, Caragh bleeding through her openings. I wince, close my eyes. But the image persists. Forgetting is an act of self-preservation, but it only lasts so long. Because memories live on, in muscle and blood and bone. Bubbling up and popping behind the eyes. I see her bleeding out on the pavement and imagine that this is the moment in which her soul spills out. All that I loved, pooling in the gutter.

I burst into Marg's room. Marg! Marg! She wakes in an ungodly fright. Gasps for breath. We need a new word! I shout. Marg shatters into tears, hyperventilating. I watch her body writhe as she struggles to breathe. Oh *fuck*. I turn and dart downstairs, grab a paper bag from the kitchen drawer and sprint back up into her room. Here, I say, breathe into this. Marg snatches it from my hand and heaves air, in and out, until her breath slows and she opens her eyes. She flicks on her bedside lamp, and I see the exhaustion in her hollowed-out cheeks. What the fuck you doing that for? I sit down beside her; she pushes me away. You can't be doing that, okay? I nod. Marg reaches for me and pulls me close to her. I bury my face into her chest. Her skin smells of talc and tobacco. I'm sorry, I mutter into her naked breast, all soft and warm against my face. Scared the shit out of me, she says, you know better than to be waking me up like that. Marg lies back on her bed, one arm outstretched, inviting me. I climb in and curl up beside her. She wraps her arm around me. Says, now what you coming in here for like that, anyway? I tell her, Stella called it a king hit, she said Caragh was king hit. And I think, we need a new word. A better word. Marg closes her eyes, kisses my cheek and whispers, I'll help you think of one tomorrow.

We're having a cuppa together in the courtyard, our naked shoulders covered in speckled light, when I say to Marg, it's got to be as violent as the act. As gruesome . . . You know? Marg nods, blowing on her tea, and says, I wonder what my Old People would say. I ask her, do you know many words in your language? This question, I see in her face, pains her, and I immediately regret asking it. Sorry, I say. She shakes her head, no, no, it's okay . . . but no, not really. I was so young when I was removed . . . but I feel them in me, even if I can't remember them. And I often think that if I heard them words again, I'd be like, oh, yeah, I already knew that. You know what I mean? I tell Marg, yeah, the body has a way of remembering. Marg smiles, that's right. She touches my hand from across the table. You're smart, you are. I feel myself blushing. I tell her, I've been thinking . . . and I think words sometimes fall short. Like they're unable to stretch, or something. Because king hit is so *wrong*. It's like words do not always represent the body, or the truth . . . Because the truth is, she was taken out for slaughter. Marg raises her eyebrows. That's it. That's exactly it. I nod my head, yeah. It is . . . Caragh was slaughter punched.

limb two

When Pearl calls me, I'm grateful that she's already heard what I've lost, that I don't have to meet her excited questions with devastating answers. There's a position open for junior editor, she says. You'll have to apply and interview, of course, but I was so impressed by you when you were my intern . . . you're the first person I've called.

I thank her and tell her I'd like to apply.

Thomas is offered a book deal with the publishing house that Han is working at. I don't know this yet when I get home from the pool and the words *I can't be with you anymore* fall out of my mouth.

He stands back. Then, after a long and aching silence, he tells me about the offer, says, maybe things will be different now.

I shake my head and say, you're not hearing me . . .

He's hated me, and rightly so, for weeks for breaking his trust. But now, confronted by the reality of me leaving, I hear his voice breaking. No, he says. No. You can't do this.

I say, it's too late, Thomas.

But I'm ready . . . I'm ready to forgive you.

I consider that another me might have folded in this moment, might have swallowed his cries and given in, might have held and rocked him and whispered in his ear, I didn't mean it, I take it back. But swimming has simplified things. Through the repetition of every tumble turn, stroke, kick and breath, all that is excess is chipped away, like rain eroding rock, until the raw truth is the only thing left.

The revelation is blisteringly painful, because the impossibility of a future together rubs up against a brimming vessel of memory, overflowing with all the still and quiet moments, all the personal jokes, all of the lovemaking and all of the maps I drew of his body, charting his terrain, a topography I knew as if it were my own . . . And it was mine, in a way . . . it was my home.

The thought of leaving, of walking into new land over the horizon, a place I don't yet know the shape of, is terrifying, but the water, I have found, carries what I can't. And at some point, between a kick and a breath, the thought of staying has become more terrifying than the thought of leaving. And this is when I know it's time. I say to him quietly, I have to . . . I have to go. I need to be alone.

And I can't explain any more of the *why* because I have no words for this feeling. Still, it's there in me, full-bodied and ready to expand, this thing I have no language for.

Where will you go? he asks.

I want to move closer to the sea.

limb one

WHAT ARE YOU writing? Marg asks as she lays a plate of Vegemite toast in front of me. I'm sitting at the outdoor table in our court-yard. The sun overhead is milky white behind a thin veneer of cloud. I'm not hungry, I tell her. Marg shakes her head. I will not have you wasting away. She takes a seat opposite me. I slide my open notebook across the table and begrudgingly pick up a piece of toast.

QUEER-ING

Queer, as in adjective,
        as in being,
        as in, I am this

Queer, as in verb,
        as in doing,
        as in, I *queer* this

Queer, as in fucking queers!

Queer, as in I Queer'd this
       as in, I made it beautiful

When Marg looks up from the page, she says, God, I hate that word. Then she sighs. And I sense that she might be about to say something else, but then she closes her mouth and slides the notebook back across the table. I take it and tell her, context will always determine the meaning of a word. And a context can be resisted . . . reorganised . . . reimagined. She shakes her head. You can get as philosophical as you like, but I will never hear that word and not feel myself getting kicked.

Queer, as in, I miss Caragh.

limb two

ON MY FIRST day working for Pearl, she takes me out for lunch. We eat laksa together at a small hole-in-the-wall restaurant by Wynyard. The spicy soup runs down our chins, bright orange. Pearl wipes her mouth with a napkin and says, I'm so glad to have you working with me. Then she raises her glass of iced tea and clinks it with mine.

I feel so relieved. These last few years . . . they've been a lot.

Pearl, with her buoyant hair, glamorous clothes and razor-thin eyebrows, sighs. She says, I heard you and Thomas parted ways.

I nod.

I also heard he got a book deal.

He did, yeah.

I didn't bid on it . . . I couldn't have you working on your ex-husband's manuscript.

Sorry that you missed out, I say, then I laugh at how surreal it all feels. I'm grateful you didn't buy it, I confess. That would have been weird.

I can be cutthroat in the boardroom, she says, but I'm not cruel. Then she asks, where are you living now?

By Gordon's Bay, I'm renting a studio apartment there. I've started swimming the bay every morning.

Pearl gasps. In a wetsuit, I presume?

I grin and shake my head. No, it's just me and my bathing suit.

You're totally mad, she says. You know that, don't you?

I get into a routine, waking each morning at first light to wriggle into my swimsuit. More often than not, it's still damp from the day before. I fill my water bottle with hot water and a wedge of lemon, which I drink as I walk along the cool and quiet street, towel slung over my shoulder, down the steep stairs, into the small sandy cove, then out onto the rock platform, fringed at the water's edge by flowing seaweeds and barnacles and sea urchins. I leave my towel and water bottle on the rocks and dive in. I have to time the dive with the rise of the swell. For the first few attempts, I missed the timing and fumbled over the scungy rocks, grazing my leg one morning on the shells. But with each attempt, I've grown more comfortable, more confident, so that now I launch into the rush of thick tide, effortless and at home.

Above the surface, the water is green grey and ruffled. Beneath, I enter the heavens, where sky erupts in blooms of algae, and schools of fish shimmer in sun-drenched waters. Occasionally, I swim over a grouper fish, slow moving and shining blue, and feel a kick of joy in my chest at the sight of these gentle giants.

Every morning, I glide through clouds of sea foam and feel warm currents caressing my body. Here, I am held, carried, strong and capable.

Afterwards, I shower until the purple has faded from my fingertips and toes. Then I brew black coffee, pour it into my thermos, grab the sandwich I prepared last night and head out the door. I catch the bus into the city, riding through Darlinghurst, with its fresh licks of paint and sidewalk cafes opening. At first, this route brings back a flood of memories, but with each trip, I slowly come to terms with them, until I no longer flinch when I remember the whole days spent in bed, Thomas and I, our young bodies coiled together, reading books to each other. Instead, I greet the memory with a smile, letting it wash through me and out, like river water.

At work, I read manuscripts for Pearl, lost all day in distant worlds, real and imagined. Sometimes, I recall my days in the school library, thinking one day one day one day I'll be a real publisher, and though the shape of this dream is different from what I'd imagined, I glow with pride, because here I am, living it.

Giulia gets a job in the nonfiction division of the same publishing house as me, and we take to sitting on the wall outside the front of the building, on the gusty streets, eating our lunches and chatting. Sometimes Han joins us. Kindly, she doesn't talk to me about the work she's doing on Thomas's book.

When I catch the bus home, I arrive as dusk settles on the horizon, everything darkening until the sky and sea become one shade of indigo and you can't tell where one ends and the other begins. I put on a record and have a bath surrounded by tealight candles. Then, all warm and tender from the water, I cook dinner in my bathrobe and eat in bed while I read. Occasionally, Gwen calls me or I call her, and we chat about what she's been knitting and I tell her what fish I've seen and what books I'm editing.

When the whales begin passing Sydney, on their journey from the Coral Sea down to Antarctica, I invite Mum and Gwen to come and whale watch with me. I take a thermos of tea, and meet them on the coastal footpath that runs between Bondi and Coogee. We walk out to the coast's edge and pause against the railing, drinking from the thermos as whales blow breath high into the sky. When the whale calves breach playfully, landing in fat sprays of water, Mum and Gwen squeal and giggle and yahoo. I smile at the voluptuous surrender.

Like this, days pass through me, or I pass through them. Either way, the transition is smooth, because when I swim, it's just my body and my mind, blurring together, until they're as inseparable as the night sky and the night sea, and I'm no longer resenting my flesh for what it couldn't become.

limb one

I CLIMB UP on stage, into the blazing lights, and the crowd becomes difficult to see. I tap the mic and hear my shallow breath beamed out through the bar. This is the first time I've performed a poem on this stage in years, but I don't tell them that. It's the fourth anniversary of Caragh's death, but I don't tell them that either. These are my secrets, and they create an atmosphere around me of *almost* knowings. It makes the performance holy, because something stays in the dark – mysterious and divine. At least, that's what Caragh would have said. Actually, I'm not sure if I agree.

I lean in towards the microphone and greet the audience, hello. I lock eyes with Dave by the bar and he gives me a thumbs up. I say, I'm going to read a few poems. This first is called, riverbend . . .

the river is punctuated with creatures
> stones and stone fish and
> almost frogs

sometimes you step on a river creature
> and the pain is long and
> unending

sometimes you try to swallow air
> but your lungs are already filled

sometimes you try to swallow her
> and you wheeze water

so, you keep her in your mouth

she is soft in your mouth
even the memory of her,
> soft in your mouth

the river bends and turns a corner, and you're carried around that corner, to a new stretch of water, punctuated by new creatures, and there is just so much ahead, just when you thought you understood, just when you thought you knew, and so you ask the river, how do I hold you?

you put your head under, and you hear the almost frog say to you, *it is impossible,*
you cannot hold a river!

you come up, head above, and laugh at the sky, because you agree with the almost frog. It still hurts, how crazy is that?

I look up, into the silence. For a long moment. And then I say, the end, even though it's not part of the poem. Because no one claps until I say, the end, and even then, the applause is timid, and confused. I take a breath and push it out. This poem, I say, is called, Queen of the Lesbians.

once, you hear a lesbian say, I don't believe in transexuals
and Daphne cries, HEAVEN FORBID, I believe in myself!
I believe *my-self*!
and you smile
you know this is true

        you know that some folks transform,
        in order to save themselves
because she told you this,
and you believe her still

There are soft murmurs in the bar at the mention of Daphne's name. Most people here won't know who she was, or who she could have become. It's a young crowd these days. A lot of university students who've read Butler and come to find us. Kids who think they know what we've lost. I hear the few stragglers who are still here and still remembering whisper, *may she rest in peace*. I clear my throat and say into the mic, okay, this one is called, coins.

Words sometimes don't stretch wide enough,

You know.

How they aren't always big enough for the whole truth.

You know,
what it feels like to live outside language.

Someone coins a new term, and then another, and another, until there's a whole drawer of gold coins, glistening and glittering, and someone else is complaining now about how the shining is hurting their eyes and it's all too much and it's all gone too far! But you know differently.

You know,
what it feels like,
to pick up that coin
           and stick it between your teeth,
             tasting the metallic tang of precision.

Because you've been starved outside, and now you're right in language.

I receive a small applause for this poem as I take a sip of water and lean back towards the microphone. Okay, I say, this last one is called, skin.

        the story of my dead friends gets richer in the retelling

so that maybe you, there, listening, might feel like you know them, too

great
belly laughing
cunt licking

great
piano playing
shit singing
great

let me tell you,

                        my dead friends were so much fun

let me tell you,
we had *so* much fun
let me tell you,

                 God,

it was worth it

I choke on this last line in a way that is both unexpected and welcomed. I stand back from the mic and take a modest bow to an audience that isn't sure what to make of my performance. I get down off stage and scan the crowd, but so few faces are familiar, so I go up to the bar, into Big Dave's arms, and Johnny passes me a whiskey on the rocks. That was good, Marg says. And I laugh. Just *good*? Marg laughs now, too, says, oh, come on! You know I don't like poetry! She playfully whips me with a tea towel. I like the last one though. Johnny smiles, glassy-eyed. Me too, he says. Then, after a long pause, he quietly adds, it really was, wasn't it . . . it was worth it.

I tell Dave I'm just ducking out for a cig and push through the crowd. At the foot of the stairs, a woman pats me on the shoulder. Hey, she says. I search her face, but I don't recognise her. Do I know you? She laughs, shakes her head. This woman is older than me, with a salt-and-pepper bob and a smart woollen coat. Her lipstick is perfectly painted on with lip-liner edges. I'm Pearl, she says, I'm a publisher. She outstretches her hand and I shake it. Nice to meet you. Yes, she says, you too. I saw you perform. You're an excellent performer. Oh, I say, thank you. I try . . . She laughs again, and I wonder if she's flirting with me. Have you ever had your work published? I shake my head. Pearl asks me, is it something you'd consider? I shrug. My poems have always been a way of speaking to my friends. I don't know, I say. Maybe? Pearl reaches into her handbag and pulls out a card. Please, she says, call me if you ever want to share any of your poems. I am about to take the card when she continues, if we could, you know, tweak them . . . just a little bit! I think your work would be very accessible to a general audience. I hesitate, the card, in her hand, hovering awkwardly between us. Perhaps you missed it, I say at last. Pearl frowns and says, I didn't mean to offend you. I assure her, trust me, you didn't. I'm just not interested.

Outside, in the biting cold, I light a cigarette and lean against the wall. I've stood out here God knows how many times in two decades, and yet, in this moment, now, with crystal clarity, I remember arriving here with Dave, and greeting my future. All of a sudden, something about this moment feels like an ending. Or like it ended already, and I missed it. Johnny comes out and pulls a pack of cigarettes from his pocket. His hands are shaking. He flicks a lighter, but it doesn't spark. Here, I say, and offer him my matchbox. Thanks, he says. He lights the end of his cigarette, inhales, exhales, sighs. Then he says, without looking at me, I'm going to sell the bar. I ask, are you serious? Even though, inside, some strange feeling at once is answered. Well, he says, it's already happened. Marg and I have sold it.

I nod, take a draw of my cigarette, blowing the smoke up towards the sky, the plume yellowed by a nearby streetlight. I need to leave, he says, the city . . . I want to be somewhere quiet. I'm sick of this racket, you know? Conversation is just noise when you're outside of it . . . I reach down and touch Johnny's hand, interlacing our fingers. His skin is smooth and cool. You have terrible circulation, I say. He squeezes my hand, says, I always have. I laugh and tell him, I know. It's the first thing I learnt about you. Right here, actually. He smirks. Darling. Surely the first thing you noticed was my fabulousness? I grin, and ask him, where will you go? North, he says. Lismore, maybe. Then he says, Dave is going to come with me. We've heard of a few guys moving up. And, well, I want to be somewhere warm.

I lean back against the wall, skull against cold brick, sucking in a lungful of night air, trying to stomach the entirety of this revelation. And it dawns on me that perhaps I can't stomach it. Because it is swollen so huge with attachments – the tears, the belly laughs, the hands held tight, the shoulders cried on, the screams, the sweat, the lovemaking, the pashes against the wall, the organising, the protesting, the care, the smiley eyes, the shouts, the singing, the poetry, the joy – and it is both heartbreaking and beautiful to know how much life we have lived here.

Big Dave comes out and finds Johnny and me still standing in the cold. I try to speak but I falter. I begin to cry, laugh, mumbling, I'll just miss you two, so much. Dave wraps an arm around me, the other around Johnny, pulling us into a tight circle.

273

Hey, he says, we're your family. And we always will be . . . Dave's voice cracks now. Then he and Johnny start crying, too, our bodies all shuddering, jolting against each other like brackish water. You better come visit us, says Johnny. I nod my head. I will, I promise, I will. You're my skin.

limb two

PEARL GOES TO New York for a book fair and comes back with
an exhibition pamphlet. I saw this before I left, she says, putting
the pamphlet down on my desk. Kiki Smith is the artist, have
you heard of her?

I open the pamphlet and feel instantly as if I've seen this
work before, though not in real life . . . the memory, I realise,
isn't mine. Because it's shared, communal even, a memory that
exceeds the boundary of one body and takes up space in a collec-
tive dream, as if her work is tapping into some primal truth I've
forgotten . . . something repressed.

Whoa, I say.

I thought you'd like it. Pearl smiles. You can keep it, she says,
then goes into her office.

I put aside the manuscript I was reading and look more
closely at the image. It's a photograph of a sculpture on the
ground in a gallery, white walls and polished concrete floors. The
sculpture is of a wolf, lying on its back, abdomen sliced open.

Out of its belly, a grown woman is stepping forward, into fresh day.

I read the curator's statement, which describes Kiki Smith's work as a revival of the Surrealist movement, drawing on motifs of fairytales, to interrogate the materiality of woman and the abjection of motherhood. I sit back in my chair and my spine clicks. I breathe out a sigh of relief.

When I get home, I put the pamphlet in my shoebox of treasured possessions, which I keep hidden beneath my bed. Kiki Smith takes up residence between seashells, my first journal, my great-grandmother's black pearl bracelet, a quill pen, the socks Gwen knitted for her granddaughter and sea eagle feathers.

limb one

We are revolting, to you,
in your eyes,
spat out of your mouth.

> We are *revolting*
> against you,
> with our joy
> unbridled

Ha! laughs Marg. I don't like poetry, she says, but I like this
one. And then she hugs me. I kiss her cheek and tell her, I'm
gonna put them all together . . . like, make a collection out of
them. I've got so many now . . . Marg asks, you gonna show
them to someone? She lets go of me and I shrug. Maybe under
a different name, I say. How about that lady from the bar? Marg
asks and I say, I didn't take her card. She pinches my cheek and

calls me a dickhead. I laugh. Then she says, you remember her name? Yeah, I say. Pearl. Well, says Marg, there can't be too many Pearl publishers around? I ponder this. Yeah, true.

Uranian House is condemned the day Marg and I find Pearl's name in the Yellow Pages. We are sitting in the courtyard and Marg says, here. She slides the thick directory across the table to me, points and says, this is the publisher's address. I write it down in my notebook. Then she looks over her shoulder and asks, can you hear that? Yeah, I say, I think someone's at the door. We walk through Uranian House, through rooms that have held our parties and our lovemaking, joy flaking off the walls, down dark corridors of pain where swellings of damp are giving way to mould, to the mouth of the house, where we open the door to two well-dressed young men in hard hats who tell us it is no longer *safe* to live here. And I suspect I won't ever be able to write the entirety of this blow to my heart, because some moments, I'm learning, are meant only to be felt. Some moments are felt so big that language cannot stretch wide enough to include it all. This, I feel, is one of those moments.

Where will you go? I ask Marg. She answers, up north. I'm going to go see Johnny and Dave in Lismore. If I like it, I might stay. They've been banging on about me moving up there for long enough. Maybe I'll finally make their day . . . She laughs, but there are tears in her eyes. Then she says, what about you? I tell her, I want to move closer to the sea.

I sleep in bed with Marg for our final night in Uranian House. I had asked her if I could spend my last night in her room, since it was where I first slept here. When we wake, I roll over and look at her, still asleep. Lukewarm light is filtering through the windows. Marg is snoring softly, and I am overcome by grief remembering how this was the sound that would usher me back to sleep during my first weeks in this house, when I would wake from a night terror, unable to remember where I was. How her breath was the anchor that settled me.

When the house is entirely empty, Marg and I walk through Uranian House one last time to check there's nothing left. As we pass through each room, we remember the lives lived in between these walls. *Goodbye,* we whisper. *Goodbye. Goodbye. Goodbye.* Until we're back at the front door, and we press our trembling palms against the wood and plaster. Whispering. *Goodbye. Goodbye, house. Thank you. We love you . . . Thank you so much.*

limb two

I DIVE INTO the ocean and begin swimming across the bay. The water today is crystal clear. It's the weekend and I slept in, so the sun is already climbing high by the time I get in the water. The wash of light makes everything underwater glow. I am swimming breaststroke when I pull water in, surface for a breath, and the memory of a girl who lived over my parents' fence catches in my throat. I put my head under, blow out my breath and see her swimming beneath me, her body gliding in rippled blue light. She is laughing, the joy leaving her body in huge green bubbles. I surface again for another breath, then put my head down, searching, but she is gone.

limb one

MY HAIR IS wet from my morning swim when I go alone to a stationery store in Bondi to buy a binder to bind together my words, and because they feel like my insides, I write a different name on the back cover. One my chosen family, my skin, won't suspect. I write the first name I was given . . . Lucy. Not as a return, but as an escape. A pseudonym, I think, is a way to detach, and therefore, a way to move forward. Beneath the name, I write the landline at my studio apartment down by the water at Gordon's Bay. I turn the binder over and across the front cover, I write the name of my collection.

Dave comes to Sydney to visit me at my new place. He arrives on Friday afternoon, two bottles of Coke in hand. His hair is washed white these days. Jesus, Big Dave, you're getting on, I tease. He laughs. Still got that tongue on you, don't you, Little Dave? He cracks open the bottles and passes one to me. It's nice to see you. We clink bottles. Yeah, he says, you too. Then he walks over to the window and takes in the sight of the ocean. How's life up north? I ask. He turns back to me and says, it's quiet. I smirk. Johnny's not carrying on like a cut snake? He shakes his head, laughing that deep belly chuckle that still feels like home. Marg is living with us. It's peaceful . . . Then he smiles and says, and she's met someone. I exclaim, what!? Dave nods his head and laughs. I reckon Marg is even more surprised by it than we are . . . But she's excited too. It's beautiful to witness, Dave says. I walk over and he slings his arm around my shoulder. We stand together and admire the sea, wide and undulating. Then he says, you know they're screening the Mardi Gras parade tomorrow on TV? I respond, yeah, I heard. He asks, are you going? I shake my head, nah, I thought we could stay here, kick our feet up? Have a cuppa? Big Dave pulls me tight against him. He whispers, yeah, that sounds good to me.

And so, we will watch the parade from my couch. And we will laugh, and we will cry, thinking of beginnings and how our skin ripped open. How our blood was an opening for this. How our bodies made this possible.

limb two

MY HAIR IS wet from my morning swim when I walk into work with my coffee in hand. I sit down at my desk as Pearl comes by with a stack of manuscripts. She puts them down on my desk and points to the one on top. This looks interesting, she says. I'm curious to know what you think.

Thanks, I say as I eye the bound pages, gauging the size of the manuscript, I should be able to get you a report by the end of the day.

Great, says Pearl before walking into her office.

I pick up the manuscript and am struck by the unusual title.

I open to the first page and read the dedication: *for Caragh.*

Then I read a poem, 'Queer-ing', and feel something turn. I read 'Riverbend' and 'Burning Histories' and 'You, as Murmurations' and 'Entrances' and 'Winter Dark' and 'Marcel' and 'Skin' and 'Queen of the Lesbians' and 'Uranian House' and 'Shame Nation' and 'I Bury A Friend' and 'Birds',

all the books speak
of butterflies, but I feel
birds in my
stomach, thick-winged and
thrashing

and feel slowly that my world is being inverted, like I've been looking at a painting, my entire life, upside down, and now the picture is suddenly clear and fully realised, abstractions taking the shape of bodies, all shiny flesh and limbs entangled. I finish the collection with tears in my eyes, breathless and aching, because here are words. Here is language. I laugh, out loud, at my desk, utterly disarmed by my joy, realising that this whole time, the picture was a portrait of two women, in love.

I flip the manuscript over and find the contact of the author handwritten on the back. I pick up the phone and punch in the number.

A man answers. Hello?

Hi, this is Suzanne. I'm calling for Lucy?

I hear the man put down the phone and speak to another person in the room. He says, someone called Suzanne . . . Maybe the wrong number? Says she's calling for Lucy.

There are murmurs passed and the muffled sounds of footsteps. Then, another voice speaks. Um . . . yes . . . Who is this?

My name is Suzanne. I'm an editor. I've just finished your manuscript, *A Language of Limbs* . . .

a language of limbs

THERE'S POETRY, YOU find, in the folds of her skin, aged and blemished by the sun, and the water. poetry in the tightening of your ribs around your lungs as you breathe her in. there's poetry, too, not in the power you are given as you enter her body, but in her giving.

you didn't know you could love like this again. so fully. so entirely. heart swollen. pulsating, red and weighted. because you meet her in a cafe by the sea and there's something in the wrinkled edges of her smile that feels like a homecoming, like your body is recognising a future in which you live, days spreading out in front of you . . .

you swim together for the first time, and find yourself opening your eyes underwater, even though it stings. you open your eyes underwater, just to see her move, her body gliding through pillars of yellow light.

when she becomes your world, you're no longer held to what's beneath you, you're pulled sideways, dragged, your body, into some other orbit. it takes you by surprise, this gravity, as you're pulled across her sky, across her skin like clouds, a river system overhead, inverted and shiny.

falling in love, you decide, is falling home. it's clumsy and awkward, utterly wonderful. you're so vulnerable in the freefall. there's so much unlearning. it's letting go of what you knew and how you used to. surrender to her gravity, to the darkness of her unknown. land there, home.

you smile at this thought and breathe into your edges, because her eyes are open sky at dawn, even when it hurts.

acknowledgements

THANK YOU, COBY Edgar (also known as Morgan Mags Marlow), Jonny Seymour, Aurora Kerr, Penny Hurndall, Led Pritchard, Felix May, Tracey Todd, Warren Roberts, and my PhD supervisor, Paul Dawson, for your close reads, consultation, and thorough notes.

Thank you, Eric Riddler at the Art Gallery of New South Wales and Ronald Briggs at the New South Wales State Library, for assisting me with early archival research. Thank you to the researchers, archivists and authors at Pride History Group whose repository of historical material and publications laid the foundations of this book. TV shows including *It's a Sin* (2021) and *Pose* (2018), films including *120 BPM* (2017), *RIOT* (2018), *Blue Jean* (2022), and *Holding the Man* (2015), and books including Jennifer L. Shaw's *Exist Otherwise: The Life and Works of Claude Cahun* (2017), Susan Stryker's *Transgender History* (2008), Shon Faye's *The Transgender Issue* (2021), Fiona Kelly McGregor's *Buried Not Dead* (2021) and Pride History Group's

New Day Dawning and *Out and About* were profoundly influential and crucial to the making of this novel. Thank you to my dear friend Jonny Seymour, who bridged entire oceans to help me view *Witches, Faggots, Dykes and Poofters* (1980) for my 30th birthday.

This is a novel about family, those that are made and those that we make for ourselves. Thank you to my family for your undying care. This novel is indebted to my early readers: Georgia, Lindy, Will, Kelly, Cloudy, Nick, Pearl, Morgan, Jehan, Felix, Claud, Shanna, Stevie, Claire, Brenna and Chloe. This novel is also indebted to Tom, Bec, Dhaksh, Yassmin, Matt, Joy, Nat, Annie, Aisha, Lola, Javi, Anton, Zoe, Louie, Imogen, Zev, Joey, Jake, Peace, Imbi, Shiri, Tesh, Lee, Cici, Risako, Honor, Babi, Louie, Di, Jessamyn, Chels, Ally, Tracey, Lily, Sav, Nevo, Madison, Roberto, Alicia, Trace, Ash, Lorcan, Gen, Sam, Robin, Emma Maye, Joseph, Danno, Alice, Rudy, Tom, Kate, Soph, Charlie, Jess, Rahnee, Rae, Ange, Greyson, Cass, Vik, Josie and everyone else from my wider family who congregate on dance floors and around dinner tables, by the water and at The Bearded Tit (thank you, Joy!!). You've all taught me that community is a verb, that it is something we do for each other.

Thank you to Benython Oldfield, Sharon Galant and Thomasin Chinnery at Zeitgeist Agency, as well as Stacy Testa at Writers House for championing this story as proudly and as relentlessly as you have. Thank you to Cate Blake, Bri Collins and the entire team at Pan Macmillan for your deep care, immense editorial work and support. Thank you also to Pilar Garcia-Brown and the entire team at Dutton (Penguin Random House) in the USA for your stellar edits, belief in my work and continued support. Thank you to Rachel Gardner, Laura Nagy,

Jo Porter and the entire team at Curio Pictures, and my manager, Josh Kesselman, for developing the screen adaptation of this novel, and in doing so, helping me to make the novel much richer and more complex.

A Language of Limbs was written as part of my PhD in Creative Writing at UNSW, which was supported through an Australian Government Research Training Program Scholarship. Thank you to the University of New South Wales staff, my supervisors and my PhD peers whose support, guidance and feedback were crucial to the making of this novel.

Thank you to those who have fought and been visible, who've cried out in both pain and pleasure, who've made radical art and who've loved bravely. It's because of you that I have been able to write and publish this book as an openly queer and transmasculine author. I love you. Thank you.

Finally, thank you to my great uncle, my Queer lineage, my inspiration and soul love, Douglas Harrs, who taught me that the role of the artist is to make things glow. Whenever I visited him in his garden, his eyes would water at my arrival, and he'd say, 'Oh, my dear, you're here. I just knew today was going to be a good day'. Douglas slipped away peacefully in his sleep only a few months before this novel was published, but I can assure you, he lives on in Uranian House, the home he so greatly inspired.

Dylin Hardcastle is a transmasculine person of Welsh and Irish settler migrant descent living on stolen and unceded Gadigal Land. Dylin is an award-winning author, artist, screenwriter and former Provost's Scholar at the University of Oxford. They are the author of *Below Deck* (2020), *Breathing Under Water* (2016) and *Running Like China* (2015). Their work has been published to critical acclaim in eleven territories and translated into eight languages. They are the cocreator, cowriter and codirector of the series *Cloudy River*, which premiered at Mardi Gras Film Festival in 2020 and was later acquired by SBS On Demand. As an artist, they have travelled to Antarctica, South America and Europe for artist residencies. In 2019, Dylin worked as a research assistant in World Literature at the University of Oxford. Their novel *A Language of Limbs* was written as part of their PhD in Creative Writing at the University of New South Wales. In 2023, *A Language of Limbs* won the Kathleen Mitchell Award through Creative Australia. The novel has been optioned by Curio (Sony Pictures) and is in development.